SHAOZHEN

THROUGH MY EYES: NATURAL DISASTER ZONES

Hotaka (Japan)

Shaozhen (China)

Lyla (New Zealand)

Angel (Philippines)

THROUGH MY EYES

Shahana (Kashmir)

Amina (Somalia)

Naveed (Afghanistan)

Emilio (Mexico)

Malini (Sri Lanka)

Zafir (Syria)

THROUGH MY EYES NATURAL DISASTER ZONES

series editor Lyn White

SHAOZHEN

WAI CHIM

ALLEN&UNWIN

SYDNEY·MELBOURNE·AUCKLAND·LONDON

First published by Allen & Unwin in 2017

Allen & Unwin
83 Alexander Street
Crows Nest NSW 2065
Australia
Phone: (61 2) 8425 0100
Email: info@allenandunwin.com
Web: www.allenandunwin.com

A Cataloguing-in-Publication entry is available from the
National Library of Australia
www.trove.nla.gov.au

ISBN 978 1 76011 379 7

For teaching resources, explore www.allenandunwin.com/resources/for-teachers

Cover and text design by Sandra Nobes
Cover photos: portrait of boy by Boris Austin/Getty; motorcycle by David Evans/
Getty; dry land by BIHAIBO/iStock; bridge by Ashley Cooper/Visuals Unlimited,
Inc./Getty.
Set in 11/15 pt Plantin by Midland Typesetters, Australia
This book was printed in June 2017 by McPherson's Printing Group, Australia.

10 9 8 7 6 5 4 3 2 1

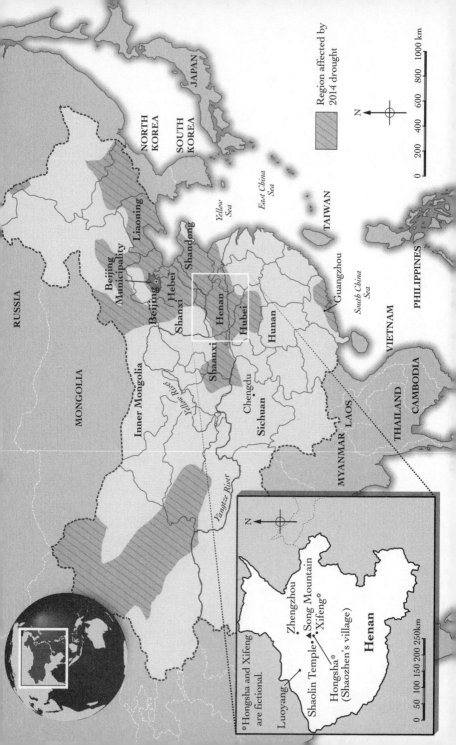

RUSSIA

MONGOLIA

Inner Mongolia

Yellow River

NORTH
KOREA

SOUTH
KOREA

JAPAN

Liaoning

Beijing
Municipality

Beijing

Hebei

Shanxi

Shandong

Yellow
Sea

East China
Sea

Shaanxi

Henan

Hubei

TAIWAN

Chengdu

Sichuan

Yangtze River

Hunan

Guangzhou

South China
Sea

MYANMAR

LAOS

VIETNAM

THAILAND

CAMBODIA

PHILIPPINES

Region affected by
2014 drought

N

0   200   400   600   800   1000 km

Henan

N

Zhengzhou

Song Mountain

Xifeng*

Shaolin Temple

Hongsha*
(Shaozhen's village)

Luoyang

*Hongsha and Xifeng
are fictional.

0   50 100 150 200 250km

One

Night had fallen over Henan and the moon was high in the sky. The road unfurled into the darkness, a dull, muted grey. Shaozhen listened to the chittering of the mosquitoes and crickets, trying his best to match their rhythm as he dribbled the basketball.

He shifted the weight of his bedding and sleeping mat from one shoulder to the other, pulling his pack, bursting with clothes and worn textbooks, closer to his body. After a long and gruelling school year, he was finally heading home for the summer. Shaozhen boarded at Xifeng Junior Middle School, like many of his class-mates, and only made the ninety-minute walk home for the weekends.

Shaozhen had mixed feelings about returning home. The market town of Xifeng had a few thousand people, a cotton mill and granary, actual restaurants and shops, while Hongsha had nothing but chickens and farmers.

At least school was over. His last exams had been brutal and his teacher had made him stay later than the rest of the students to complete an additional assignment. 'You need all the extra marks you can get,' Master Chen had observed.

Shaozhen definitely wouldn't miss the schoolwork. Unlike when he had gone to primary school, junior middle school was very difficult and he had to study night and day just to keep up. Over the past four weeks, Master Chen had insisted he stay at school over the weekend for extra tutoring instead of going home. He had been stuck in a dingy classroom with just two other boys, cramming for exams until he thought his brains would burst.

But that was finally over and Shaozhen was free. He had better ways to spend his time than solving maths problems or reading boring history books. Like playing basketball.

Thunk. Thunk. Thunk. Even with the heavy pack weighing him down, Shaozhen moved nimbly with the basketball. He practised lay-ups, dribbling and drills all the way home. He imagined himself as his idol, the greatest basketball legend in China: Yaoming. Shaozhen would sometimes fantasise about life as a player in the NBA – flying in private jets, signing autographs, making friends with the greats, the enormous crowds cheering him on.

Thunk. Thunk. Thunk. The ball struck the hard dirt of the road that led to Hongsha, one of eight small villages surrounding Xifeng that were set in the valley of the Song mountains. Near Xifeng, the main road was paved, lined with humble shops, apartment blocks and some small houses. As he got closer to his village, the shops and houses gave way to sprawling fields and farmland.

On the other side of Hongsha, the road wound up the looming mountains and past some of the most remote villages of Henan, dotted along the mountainsides. Beyond those mountains lay the province of Shanxi. While the villagers went into Xifeng often, there was little reason to venture up the mountains and deeper into the countryside – they were removed enough as it was.

Hongsha seemed deserted when Shaozhen strode through the concrete gate with the words 'Hongsha Village, Xifeng Township' emblazoned in dull brass letters across the top. It was home to just under fifty families, most of them farmers. The village's three shops were closed for the day, the primary school was silent, and there was a padlock across the iron bars in front of the village headquarters.

As he walked towards home, Shaozhen could hear chatter and laughter coming from the houses, rising above the loud and constant barking of some village dog. The weather was unseasonably warm, and many of the villagers were spending their evening outside on their stoops. Shaozhen weaved through the alleys. He nodded at the two old women squatting down and gossiping as they peeled vegetables and mashed ganshu, sweet potato, in a large bowl. He hurried past the billowing of smoke coming from a group of old men, smoking cigarettes and swapping stories in the dim moonlight.

Shaozhen turned the corner and stepped into the darkness of the tree-lined path that led home; the bright white light from his house beckoned at the end. A slight rustling came from one of the trees. He stopped in his tracks and pivoted slowly, seeking out its source.

A small form rocketed out of the trees and almost knocked Shaozhen off his feet.

'Shaozhen, gege, big brother!' The boy barely came to Shaozhen's waist. He gazed up at him with big round eyes and wrapped his arms around Shaozhen's skinny legs.

Shaozhen laughed and handed the boy his basketball, then picked him up and tossed him over his shoulder so that Xiaoping's head dangled upside down across his back.

'Wah, wow, Xiaoping! You're getting heavy, little man!' The boy shrieked with delight as Shaozhen took off. He carried Xiaoping to the end of the path and deposited him on the ground.

'Are you being good for Aunty Wu?'

The boy nodded.

'High five,' Shaozhen offered, and Xiaoping slapped him on the palm before scampering back up the path. Shaozhen smiled and turned back to the line of houses. They were set away from the main residences in the village at the base of a hill. When Shaozhen had been young, the cluster of five families had formed their own mini-community in the village. But over the years the other houses had emptied as their residents moved away and their little cluster had diminished to just his family and Aunty Wu's.

Hot steam drifted from the vent cut into the roof of the humble hut that Shaozhen called home. His house had thick, strong walls and a high-quality tile roof, which his family was particularly proud of. Shaozhen didn't care for the tiles, but he was pleased that he had a room of his own. His father had built an extension when Shaozhen had turned eight after saving enough money for the materials. He had spent most of the New Year holiday stacking mud bricks and sealing up holes, working well into the night so that Shaozhen could have his own room by the morning.

Shaozhen had been ecstatic when his father showed the room to him. It was only wide enough to fit a single bed, with a small window looking out over the pigpen, but Shaozhen didn't mind any of that, it was a room of his very own. He whooped and hollered like he had won the NBA finals. But before he even finished moving his few belongings into his new room, his father had taken his bags and rushed to catch the midday train back to Guangzhou so he could start work again the next morning.

Shaozhen quickened his pace, his arms looping the basketball behind his back. The sound of voices and clanking dishes could be heard from inside the mud walls. 'Ma must be making something delicious,' he thought and his stomach rumbled in agreement.

'Lu Shaozhen.' Aunty Wu was sweeping the front step of her house, two doors to the right.

'Aunty Wu. Wah, what a modern haircut!' Her white hair was done up in a fresh perm that she would have gotten in Pingdingshan, the closest 'prefecture-level' city to Hongsha. Aunty Wu was one of the few villagers who ever journeyed further than Xifeng.

She patted her head with pride. 'You know how to make an old lady feel good.' At fifty-five, Aunty Wu was actually one of the younger members of the village and she was still tough as the strongest niu, ox. 'You're done with school?' she asked.

'Until next year!' Shaozhen declared, putting on a confident smile. The year had been particularly challenging and he hoped he had passed and could move on to the next level. He tried to forget Master Chen's stern face and warning. There would be nothing more embarrassing than getting left behind by his peers. His best friend, Kang, had been smarter than everyone in their grade. He'd already advanced to the next level and was now one year ahead of Shaozhen.

A squeal of laughter came from the path where Xiaoping was hiding among the trunks of the tall native plane trees.

'Xiaoping is getting big.'

Aunty Wu pressed her lips into a thin line as she watched her grandson play. 'He is. By the time his parents come back to visit, he'll be so big, they won't even recognise him,' she said in a sombre tone.

Shaozhen swallowed. Xiaoping was just three years old. *How long has it been since he's seen his ma and ba?*

'You're a lucky boy, Shaozhen.' Aunty Wu wiped the sweat from her brow. 'Your ma and nainai take good care of you. Don't forget it.'

'I won't, Aunty.' He bid Aunty Wu farewell and hurried to his door.

'Ma! Nainai! I'm back!' Shaozhen threw the door open with a sharp bang, sending a gust of wind through the room.

'Aiyah, oh my, shut the door, you silly egg! All the food will get cold.' The shrill scolding came from a lanky, rail-thin girl around his age.

'Don't be such a sourpuss, Yangyang,' Shaozhen retorted, stomping into the room as he bounced the ball in front of him, nearly knocking over the wobbly stand that held the family TV.

'Baobei, precious son, you're home.' The gentle, soothing voice belonged to Ma. Her stout form was hunched over the muhuolu, wood-burning stove, that stood next to an ice chest set up in the corner of a cluttered room; this served as the cooking area. In addition to the stand with the TV, the only furniture in the room was a single lumpy lounge chair and a wooden cabinet with a glass door that held a few framed pictures. A small folded table with a stack of wooden stools in front of it was pushed up against the wall. There was a tower of plastic basins that Ma kept for washing up. A lone fluorescent tube flickered from the ceiling, the single source of electric light in their modest home.

'Did you pass all of your exams?' Ma asked. 'Master Chen said you had a lot of catching up to do.'

Shaozhen could sense the urgency in Ma's voice. He tried not to grimace. 'I guess so. I won't know for a couple more weeks.'

His mother's face crumpled but she forced a smile. 'I hope you thanked Master Chen for all the extra time he put in.'

Shaozhen shrugged, hoping she would drop the subject, and peered over her shoulder, more interested in the delicious smell of the cooking. 'Mutton?' His mouth was already watering. He loved his ma's cooking. As far as he was concerned her yucai was the best in all of Henan.

'Your favourite.' She used a short metal spoon to stir the sauce in the pan. She pushed away a few loose strands of her blunt-cut hair before tasting the sauce, then held the spoon out to her son.

Shaozhen licked the sauce; it was tangy with a bit of fire, just the way he liked it. He smiled wide and Ma's bright eyes crinkled with satisfaction.

She checked the crackling wood burning beneath the stove then began scooping rice out of their electric rice cooker, one of the many gifts that Shaozhen's father had brought them from the city.

'Wah, what's the special occasion?' Shaozhen asked. The Lu family usually ate noodles, not rice, because they were cheaper and easier to prepare.

'Your homecoming of course, my emerging scholar. You haven't been home for a few weeks,' Ma said gently as she ladled rice into the chipped bowls. Shaozhen bristled with pride. 'And…I have some news. Big news. But for now, help Yangyang set up the table.'

Two

Shaozhen gripped the edge of the folding table and dragged it into the middle of the room, the legs scraping against the packed earth floor. Yangyang took the four bowls that Ma had laid out and placed them around the table, one on each side. Shaozhen grabbed the stools while Yangyang added a neat pair of kuaizi, chopsticks, to each setting.

'Wah. What a feast.' Nainai, Shaozhen's paternal grandmother, emerged from the room she shared with Yangyang. Ma and Ba had the third bedroom, but Shaozhen's father only came home for the New Year holidays once a year.

Nainai came over and pinched Shaozhen on the cheek with her bony fingers. 'Like a dumpling. Too much studying has made you soft, Shaozhen.' The teen made a face but knew better than to respond. Nainai was small in stature but her fury was known to rival the biggest monsoons.

'Aunty,' Yangyang said to Shaozhen's mother,

'I've finished setting the table. Here, let me help you with the rest of the food.' The girl brushed past Shaozhen, pausing to stick her tongue out at him on her way to the stove. He made a face to her back. Like many of the village children, Shaozhen was an only child and he was mostly grateful for it – imagine if he had a sibling like Yangyang!

Ting Yangyang had moved in with the Lu family just after winter last year. She'd come all the way from Sichuan, two provinces over, after her last grandmother had passed away. Yangyang's parents were migrant workers in the same factory as Shaozhen's father. When Ma had heard about the Ting family's misfortune, she had immediately offered to help. 'In this day, with all the parents in the cities and the children at home, family is more important than ever. Without family, how is anyone supposed to survive?' She had made Yangyang part of their family, and was now raising her alongside her own son. Her parents wrote Yangyang the occasional letter and she had visited them in the city once, but she never seemed to miss them.

Since she'd arrived with her bundles of belongings and messy plaits, Yangyang had done her best to make herself useful around the Lu house, helping with the chores and even out in the fields. She called Shaozhen's ma 'Aunty' and his nainai 'Laobo'. She chose not to study, even though Ma had done her best to coax her into middle school with Shaozhen. 'What can't I learn from the land and life experience?' she had challenged.

To Shaozhen, Yangyang was more than strange. She spoke a different dialect and her skin was much, much darker than that of any of the other girls from the village. She moved differently too, like a niu, not a girl. Sometimes, Shaozhen and the other boys teased her. He'd noticed her feet were flat and her toes splayed out, like webbing on a frog. Shaozhen told Kang and some of the others to call her 'Frog Feet', just to annoy her, but she didn't seem to care.

'You're such a good helper, Yangyang.' Ma was balancing the plate of mutton and another plate of vegies in her worn, knobby hands. 'I don't know what I would do without you. Shaozhen, be a good boy and help carry some plates.'

It was his turn to stick his tongue out at Yangyang as he made his way into the cooking area. She rolled her eyes.

Yangyang placed the simple dishes down on the table. In addition to the braised mutton, there were some ludou, green beans, and huangdouya, soybean sprouts, stir-fried and topped with cong, spring onions, and a bowl of lajiao, chilli, on the side. Being from Sichuan, Yangyang liked her food spicy while the rest of the family preferred a milder taste. The four of them sat at the table and Shaozhen snapped his chopsticks together, feeling ravenous.

'Wah, Lu Shaozhen, your mother spoils you rotten. You always pick the best cuts for yourself. The rest of us just eat gristle.' Yangyang remarked as she watched him pinch meat onto his bowl. 'Do they teach you manners in school?'

Shaozhen went red in the face. 'You're so ugly, like a toad,' he retorted. 'You're never going to find a husband.'

Yangyang just smiled and plunged her chopsticks into the food, picking up a few juicy pieces of mutton to pile onto Nainai's bowl. Yangyang never reacted to anything Shaozhen said, no matter how nasty he tried to be.

'You're going to have to be extra kind to each other, from now on. I have something to tell you,' said Ma.

Shaozhen was slurping ludou into his mouth but he stopped. The vegetable hung from his lips like tentacles. He swallowed them quickly. 'What is it?' He felt a tightness in his stomach and it definitely wasn't from the delicious food.

Ma sighed and set her chopsticks down. She looked from Shaozhen to Yangyang to her mother-in-law and then back to Shaozhen. 'I'm joining Ba in Guangzhou. There's a new position in the factory and they're willing to give me a trial.' She forced a smile. 'It pays thirty fen an hour. That's good money.'

A lump formed in Shaozhen's stomach and he hastily shoved some huangdouya into his mouth. His mother was leaving.

He wasn't that surprised. It wasn't the first time she had gone to the city for work. The last time she'd left, he'd just been seven years old and she'd gone to Chengdu to be a cleaner at the public bathhouses. But she had gotten very sick, an infection from the chemicals, and her leg had swollen to twice its size, thick with pus. She had come home after just three months and she'd hugged Shaozhen so tight he could hardly breathe, promising him that she would never leave again.

Of course, that was six years ago and he was much older now. He knew he should be okay with his mother's decision. Because of the rules of hukou, the national residency system, lots of children were left behind in the villages with their elderly grandparents. In fact, his ma was one of the only mothers still left in the village. Most of his friends' parents had left for the city years ago, including his best friend Kang's. Shaozhen hadn't been 'left-behind' to grow up on his own, like Kang or Xiaoping.

He remembered Aunty Wu's remark: *'You're a lucky boy, Shaozhen.'*

Right now, he wasn't too sure she was right.

'That's very good money,' Yangyang said. 'Per hour is better than when they pay per piece.' Yangyang's parents had spent a good three years working at different factories in Guangzhou before they had arrived at the garment factory that Shaozhen's father worked at.

'The harvest isn't looking so plentiful this year. It will be better if I work,' Ma said.

'Yes, it will. There hasn't been rain in months,' Nainai complained. 'We're not going to have much of a harvest. The young people are all leaving, and this village is as good as dead.'

'Hush, Popo. Let's not be dramatic.' There was no mistaking the worry in Ma's expression. But she smiled again and looked at her only son.

'What do you think, Shaozhen?' she asked softly.

Shaozhen set his kuaizi down beside his bowl and gazed at his mother. 'Guangzhou's a long way away,' he said with his mouth full. 'It's almost a day's travel by train.'

'Nineteen hours. Your ba says the city is crowded and dirty, worse than Chengdu,' she added with a frown. 'But the money will be nice. Maybe we can send you to a top-ranked senior school or even university. Imagine that!'

Shaozhen lowered his head and returned to his food.

'Well?' She laid a hand on his wrist. Her eyes were big and round, her expression beseeching.

Shaozhen gave his mother a small smile. 'I think you should go. You can keep Ba company. I know he misses you.' He ignored the knot in his stomach and grinned. 'Maybe I can visit sometime.'

His mother looked relieved. 'Of course you can,' she said as she squeezed his arm.

'When do you leave?' he asked.

'Tomorrow morning,' was her strained reply.

They ate the rest of the meal in silence.

Three

The next morning, Shaozhen refused to be sad. His mother had found a job in the city and she could be with his father. They would have more money and that meant he might be able to continue with school. Then he wouldn't have to be a farmer and be stuck in the village forever. This was all good, so why was there this niggling knot in the pit of his stomach?

Ma was up before sunrise, packing the battered suitcase with the broken wheel that his father had left behind. 'I'll have to get a new one in the city for when I visit. I'll be bringing lots of presents,' she said to her son, trying to lighten the mood. She folded up the few sets of clothes that she owned. With a couple of pairs of shoes, a frayed towel and toiletries, they barely took up half the space in the suitcase.

Nainai had stayed up all night preparing her son's favourite foods. She'd wrapped paper plates in plastic wrap and stacked them in a bag. 'The city is too busy. You two won't have time to cook,' she said as she knotted the bag at the top and shoved it into Ma's hands. The handles at the top of the bag were uneven so the bottom plate was slanted. The whole thing smelled like garlic. Shaozhen wondered how Ma would keep it from tipping over in the train.

Ma hugged Nainai and Yangyang. 'Take care of my Shaozhen,' she instructed them both.

Usually, Shaozhen squirmed in protest whenever his ma tried to hug him. This time, he stood stiffly as his mother wrapped her soft arms around him and squeezed him so tightly he thought his ribs would crack.

'Be good, my baobei. I will call and write whenever I can.'

Shaozhen felt his lower lip tremble. 'Take care of Ba,' he finally managed.

And she was off, a jacket tied around her thick waist, the wonky wheel rattling as she dragged her suitcase down the path, Nainai's bag of pungent food balanced precariously on top.

🔶🔶🔶

Feeling a bit unstuck, Shaozhen grabbed his basketball from his bedroom, hoping he could find some friends and set up a game.

He went up the tree-lined path from his home to the heart of the village. A few chickens skittered between the houses, bobbing their heads. The maze of alleyways was abuzz with villagers going about their day. Most of the able-bodied farmers had gone to their fields. The ailing elderly were left to tend to the small private gardens scattered throughout the village.

'One, two, three, four…' The rhythm and bounce of the ball was soothing and Shaozhen counted out each step. He liked to be in control, to feel the familiar texture of the rubber on the pads of his fingers, knowing what force the ball would bounce back with and how to send it hurtling to the earth once again. Everything was predictable and he didn't have to pretend he was okay.

He focused on the ball, trying to erase the image of Ma leaving, broken suitcase in tow. But it didn't work. In his mind, she was still heading out the door, slipping away, and his feet moved swiftly to follow, dribbling faster.

Shaozhen was running now, his shoes pounding the earth, sending up dust. He ran until he felt like he had left a bit of his uneasiness somewhere far behind him.

As he rounded a corner near the centre of the village, he spotted a thin boy in pants that were far too short for him. The boy was rolling up the door to a rickety wooden shack that sat among a cluster of houses. Shaozhen smiled and rushed over.

'Kang!'

His friend turned, pushing his thick spectacles up his nose. 'Shaozhen.' The glasses were cracked at the bridge and held together with bits of twine. Kang was the only person Shaozhen knew in the village who needed to wear glasses.

'Kang, let me help you,' Shaozhen said, as he reached up to unfurl the faded red awning that hung over the doorway to the shop. He noticed Kang had his school backpack, the corner of a worn book poking out the zippered front. 'Wah, Kang, we just finished school and you're *still* studying?'

Kang shrugged. He was used to being teased about his bookish ways. He went into the shop, grabbing a broom and using the handle to push up the flimsy awning, then secured it by wrapping a piece of twine around a rusty nail. 'I like reading,' he said simply. 'Besides, I have a lot to do if I'm headed for senior school next year.'

'Aw, come on, I was just saying you need a break. Don't want to hurt that big head of yours.' Shaozhen felt bad. Their mothers were best friends as well and they had started playing together when they were Xiaoping's age. They had spent hours on elaborate games: Shaozhen would pretend to be an imperial warrior and Kang, the emperor's scholar. Together the two boys had saved China from warlords and foreign invaders countless times.

But then Kang's parents had gone to nearby Zhengzhou, and later all the way to Beijing for work. They were back in Chengdu now, but they rarely saw their only son. Shaozhen had noticed his friend change: Kang stopped laughing and playing games with him. He'd had been left under the watchful eye of his strict gung, grandfather, Lao Zhu, who didn't have time for fun. He was in poor health and couldn't work in the fields, so he had opened a xiaomaibu, corner store, instead. There was already a general store and a snack shop in Hongsha, the only established businesses, and unfortunately the pair didn't sell much. For the most part, they relied on a tiny vegetable patch for food, along with the money that Kang's parents sent them every month.

Kang moved a display of packaged snacks and potato sticks, Dabaitu brand candies and instant noodles, up to the front of the store. Shaozhen was pretty sure the same ones had been hanging from the hooks since Lao Zhu had first opened the shop eight years ago. The rest of the shelves held sacks of fertiliser, two shiny wheelbarrows and dusty farm tools.

'Where's your gung?' Shaozhen asked, peering into the cramped shack.

'He had business in Xifeng.'

Shaozhen's eyes lit up. 'Hey, that's great! We can have a game of one on one. I'll teach you some moves.' Kang had never really cared for basketball, but Shaozhen was hoping that he could be persuaded.

'Nah, I have to look after the shop.' Kang grabbed a plastic stool, set it beside the display of snacks and reached for his backpack.

'Come on,' Shaozhen whined. 'You can close up for a few hours. How would your gung even know?'

Kang shrugged. He settled onto the stool and grabbed his book out of his bag. 'He'll know. He always does.' He opened the thick book and started to read.

'What are you studying?'

'Physics,' Kang said without looking up. 'The headmaster lent me the book for next year. If I get ahead, I can probably go to senior school in the city. He said if I'm good enough I might even get a scholarship.' He lost himself in his book, leaving his friend standing awkwardly outside.

Shaozhen toyed with the ball, passing it back and forth between his cupped palms. 'My mother left this morning,' he blurted out. 'She's gone to Guangzhou with my father.' He laughed nervously. 'I guess that makes me a left-behind now, like you.'

Finally, Kang lifted his head. His huge round eyes blinked behind his thick lenses and he frowned. 'I'm sorry.' His words were tender and heartfelt.

Shaozhen took a deep breath. He opened his mouth a few times, but no words came out so he just shrugged.

'Okay, book nerd,' Shaozhen said, 'I hope you get your scholarship.' He walked away. That weird feeling in the pit of his stomach was back. He had been looking forwards to finishing school and spending more time playing basketball than hitting the books, but Ma's sudden departure had changed all that. Shaozhen gritted his teeth and dribbled the ball so hard that at one point it sailed into the air above his head and he missed the rebound.

The basketball court in the village consisted of a simple hoop that had been placed next to the village headquarters alongside a concrete picnic table. There were also some benches and a lone street lamp. These had all been installed only a few years ago. The Village Secretary had called it the Party's great social endeavour, to ensure the local villagers had a recreational space to pass their time. Nainai had complained that it was only ever used by the old men to play mahjong well into the early hours of the morning.

This morning, the picnic table and the court were both empty. Shaozhen lobbed a few lay-ups and practised shooting some free throws. His eyes followed the movements of the ball as he analysed the court and mapped out potential plays and strategies, as if he were playing an actual game. Basketball made him feel completely at ease; it was a game he understood in every fibre of his being.

He bent his knees and squared his shoulders, his gaze homing in on the lip of the rim, that sweet spot against the backboard that would allow his shot to cascade down into the hoop.

A rattle and a trundle – and the ball went in. There was no net but Shaozhen could still imagine the swish.

And the crowd goes wild! Shaozhen threw his fists into the air. He waved to his pretend fans, and hummed the tune that the Americans had created for the NBA star Yaoming, and sang his own name.

Shaozhen. Shaozhen. Shaozhen. Shaozhen. Shaozhen.

'Shaozhen!' That wasn't a voice in his head. It was his nainai, calling to him from the road. Her thin limbs moved with brisk purpose, her mouth corkscrewed into a frown.

'What do you think you're doing, loafing about?' Nainai was just over seventy, and despite her petite frame she still had a stern demeanour and a shrill voice that could evoke obedience from even the most stubborn niu.

She stormed over to Shaozhen and reached up to him with a bony hand.

'Ow!' Shaozhen tried to twist away as she latched onto the lobe of his ear. But Nainai held firm as she scolded him.

'Your mother spoiled you rotten. Her baobei never had to lift a finger in the house as long as he studied. Well, not anymore!' She marched back to the road, dragging Shaozhen with her.

'Ow! Nainai, that hurts!'

His protests were ignored. She pulled Shaozhen through the alleyways in the village, past houses and gardens. A few curious heads poked out of the windows to see the boy being admonished by his grandmother. Shaozhen felt his face getting hot as he listened to the villagers sniggering at him.

'Nainai, please,' he said feebly, but she didn't let go until they were almost at the main road that led out of the village.

'That hurts.' Shaozhen rubbed his ear but it was more his ego and his pride that needed soothing.

Nainai scoffed. She began picking up tools from a pile that she must have left by the roadside before she had gone to fetch him.

'I won't have you lazing about,' she said. 'Your whole generation lives in the clouds, your heads messed up with silly dreams. You haven't done a day's worth of hard work in your life. Meanwhile, your parents are slaving away in the city.' She thrust a hoe into Shaozhen's hands. 'This stops today. Your grandfather was a farmer and his grandfather before him. I don't care what your mother says. You're going to learn how to be a farmer too.'

Shaozhen was about to point out that the real jobs were in the city. That he was in school and even if he didn't love studying as much as Kang, he might still be able to go to senior school if he made the grades, even university. All of this was at the tip of his tongue but when he looked into his nainai's eyes, his protests and arguments fell away.

'I've already lost my only son to the city,' she said, her eyes shining. 'I'm not going to let it take my only grandson too.'

Shaozhen had no words, so he just nodded. However he felt about his mother leaving, his grandmother was feeling worse. There was nothing more to say. He fell into obedient step behind her as she headed for the fields.

Four

Shaozhen felt the sting of the hot sun on his back as they climbed the short hill to the Lu family plot, a few hundred metres outside the village perimeter. There were no signs or markers; the only way to know which portion of land was maintained by which family was through the collective memory of the village history.

Hongsha had always been a farming community. The families were self-sustaining, growing their food in personal gardens in and around the village – but many of them also farmed larger plots of land with commercial crops.

Shaozhen's yeye had looked after their plot until he had passed away when Shaozhen was seven years old. Since then, Nainai had been the one tending to it every day. Shaozhen admired his grandmother's strong will. She worked harder than some of the men from the village. Nainai was the one who hooked the skinny old niu to the plough and whipped it down the rows to loosen the earth and then plant the seeds. She was the one who mixed manure and compost to create their homegrown fertiliser to help the crops grow tall. She was the one who led the niu into town and came back with bags of chemical fertiliser when their homegrown variety wasn't strong enough to make the crops thrive. And, every year, she was the one who led the other farmers to harvest the crops and set fire to the leftover stalks, clearing the fields so they would be ready for planting once again.

The money the Lu family made from the harvest was meagre but it was the only money they could make as farmers. In Hongsha, corn and other crops were sold to the government because it offered the best money per bushel. But it was still never enough. The villagers who didn't have extra income sent from family members working in the city needed to rely on their harvest money to pay for everything from school fees to doctor's bills, fabric for clothes, supplies for repairing farming equipment and for any food that they couldn't grow on the land. As a result, money was always tight.

Shaozhen's ma and ba had both helped Nainai in the fields before they left for the city, but they had acted mostly as farmhands, letting Nainai make the decisions about the land. In addition to the crops they grew to sell to the government, the Lu family raised a few pigs, which they kept in a pen outside the back of their house. The pigs were fattened up and then sold for slaughter in time for the New Year.

Shaozhen remembered doing farm work when he was younger and hating every minute of it. He had complained and whined until his mother sent him home.

When he started school, he made sure he had his nose buried in a book anytime Nainai suggested that he pick up a plough or a rake to help in the fields. His mother adored her son and always said studying took precedence over everything and Nainai would have to let the field work go.

But his mother wasn't here anymore. Shaozhen was going to have his turn as a serious farmhand for the very first time. He recalled the traditional images of the hardworking peasants he'd seen in his Chinese history textbooks and he tried to imagine himself in their shoes, but the image left him feeling sad and defeated. He didn't know what he wanted for his future, but he was certain that he didn't want to be a hunchbacked farmer all his life.

When they reached the top of the hill, Shaozhen saw that Yangyang was already out in the fields, her lump of dark hair poking out from underneath a dingy straw hat brim. She was bent double, seesawing back and forth, her shrill voice cutting through the air as she worked the ground beneath her with the same tenacity as a Shaolin monk in training.

'Hyah! Hyah! Hyah! Hyah! Hyah!'

Shaozhen couldn't help but smirk at her little cries. She was just too strange.

'Don't be so cheeky,' Nainai remarked, as though tapping into his thoughts. 'You'd learn a thing or two from her if you weren't such a layabout.'

Shaozhen felt his cheeks burning hot. He looked around the field at the short plants. 'Why are there yams out here? I thought we had planted corn.'

Yangyang sniggered. 'Are you kidding me, peanut brain? This *is* the corn!'

His jaw dropped as he surveyed the scene. The plants were brown and dry, their leaves limp and split down the middle. Shaozhen knew the corn plants should be lush and green by now, the stalks towering above their heads. But these plants barely came up to his shoulders. And it wasn't just a few rows or only their field. As Shaozhen gazed towards the horizon, he saw the tops of the farmers' heads poking out over their crops. Their fields were just as dry and just as bare.

Shaozhen swallowed the uneasy lump in his throat. 'What happened?' He regretted the words the moment they left his mouth.

His grandmother snorted. 'What do you think? It doesn't rain, crops dry up. It's been one of the driest seasons I can remember.' She set her tools down and pointed. 'We were due to irrigate last week but the stream has run dry. If the rains don't come soon, there'll be nothing to harvest.'

Shaozhen was speechless. It had been an unseasonably warm start to summer and he couldn't remember the last rains. At school the water pump was dry and they'd had to ration the drinking water in the last weeks of the term. Some of the girls at school had saved bottles of water to take home to their families. But when he asked, Ma had told him not to worry, that everything was fine and that he should focus on his upcoming exams.

Dry conditions weren't unusual for Henan. The region had had a water shortage only a few years back, and since there was no rain the farmers had relied on irrigating. But now, standing in the pittance of crops, Shaozhen realised that things had become dire. Had his mother been lying?

'Come on,' Nainai snapped, 'stop daydreaming. If there's any hope for this village, we're going to need to work harder. Start digging up the weeds.' She gestured down the rows with sweeping arms.

Shaozhen picked up his hoe. He brought it over his head then snapped the blade towards the hard ground.

Thunk.

He felt the shock of the impact through his arms and winced. His stroke had barely made a dent. He raised his arms, ready to strike again.

'Not so close to the stalks, give the plants room to breathe,' Nainai commanded.

Shaozhen grunted. He struggled to control the long shaft, to make it obey.

Thunk.

Up and down the rows they went, their tools eventually hitting the ground in synchronised rhythm. As he settled into the monotony of field work, Shaozhen's mind slipped into a trance. Unlike when he was playing basketball, there was no fluidity, no instinct in his movements. The work was just dull and tiring. And it went on and on and on until his arms felt ready to fall off his body.

'Nainai, is there any water?' His throat was bone dry.

His grandmother laughed. 'Shaozhen, don't you know what happens during a drought?'

The next morning Shaozhen stumbled to breakfast. His entire body ached, as if had been pulled apart and reassembled the wrong way. His limbs felt like they were filled with lead, his back was twisted and bent, and he could feel two thick knots at the base of his spine. He stared bleary-eyed at the bowl of soup noodles that Nainai put in front of him.

'Eat up, Shaozhen!' she commanded. 'We need to get out early and check for bugs.'

Shaozhen stifled a groan. He had never worked this hard in his life. He longed for Ma: the most she ever made him do was feed the pigs or fix things around the house.

'Yangyang, you'd better eat quickly. You need to fetch water,' Nainai groused.

'I'll do it!' Shaozhen said. *Anything to get out of working in the fields.* 'I'll get the water, no problem.'

Yangyang narrowed her eyes. 'You hate fetching water. What are you trying to pull?' she asked suspiciously.

This was true, but he was tired of field work. 'Nothing at all.' He turned his palms up, trying to appear innocent. 'I just want to help.'

Nainai grunted with what he hoped was a sign of approval.

Shaozhen wolfed down the rest of his breakfast.

'Buckets are outside,' Nainai said. 'Be sure to take both poles with you and fill up what you can.'

Both poles? Shaozhen's eyebrows shot up in confusion, but he didn't object.

He went outside and found two bamboo poles laid out by the side of the house. They had plastic buckets with long bamboo handles hanging from each end. The buckets were large, capable of carrying maybe twenty or thirty litres each. He surveyed them uneasily, before hoisting one of the poles onto his shoulders. He was under instruction to take both, but surely he could just come back for the other?

The village had a number of wells and water cellars spread out among the dirt roads, and a few outside the main entrance, closer to the farms. Fetching water was just one of the many daily tasks of village life that Shaozhen didn't mind missing out on when he was at school.

Shaozhen went to the well at the end of the tree-lined path. He pulled off the lid and peered down into the pitch blackness. The opening was just bigger than his torso. The first time he had fetched water, he had been so small that if he'd leant over just a bit too far he'd have plummeted into the well's depths.

There was a thick rope coiled neatly by the side of the well. Shaozhen attached one of the buckets to its end and sent it down. He kept feeding more and more rope in as he waited for the tell-tale splash.

'Lu Shaozhen!' A familiar voice called out to him and he spun around.

'Headmaster Song!'

A large hat obscured the man's face, but there was no

mistaking the short figure coming towards him. Song was the village primary school's headmaster; he was no taller than some of his oldest pupils but he was highly respected among the villagers. He was educated and though he had missed out on going to university, he had completed a vocational degree. As a result, he had been selected as the head of the village committee. The committee had no real say in governing affairs, that was purely the responsibility of the officials of the Communist Party of China, but Song and the rest of the committee did their best to express the interests and wishes of the Hongsha villagers to the Party leaders.

The headmaster lumbered towards him and smiled. 'Shaozhen, it's good to see you. Are you preparing for your studies for next year?'

'No, sir. It's the break.'

'Ah, I see.' The headmaster removed his hat and Shaozhen stared down at the shiny bald spot on the top of his head. 'Your classmate, Kang, asked me for some books, to get ahead. I gave him my graduate level texts and he's already halfway through them.'

Shaozhen didn't like to be reminded that he wasn't as studious as his friend and that his mother's dreams of him becoming a scholar were likely in vain. He tried to shrug off the feeling of discomfort and peered down into the well.

The headmaster must have taken pity on him, because he dropped the subject. 'How's your family? Your ma and nainai?'

'Ma left for the city. She's gone to join my father.'

Shaozhen shook the rope, wondering if the bucket was caught on something.

'Is that so?' The headmaster sounded surprised. 'I didn't realise. I'm sorry, Shaozhen.' His voice was soft and he rubbed the bald dome on his head, a pained expression on his face.

'It's no big deal, really,' Shaozhen said with a shrug. 'I'm not a little kid like Xiaoping.' He yanked at the rope again. 'Nainai said I had to help in the fields now that Ma's not here. I have to fetch water this morning too.'

Headmaster Song frowned. 'But, Shaozhen, you're not going to get any water from there. The wells have dried up. Haven't you heard? It's the worst drought in over fifty years.'

Shaozhen felt his face heating up again. He hadn't considered there might be no water in the wells. Where had his family been getting their water from?

When Shaozhen didn't respond, the headmaster continued, 'Try the well outside the village. It should still have some water in it, but we don't know for how much longer.' He looked up at the clouds. 'Not much we can do about it, I'm afraid, except pray to the ancestors. We are at the mercy of the skies.'

Shaozhen thanked the headmaster and Song walked off, plopping the hat back on his head. With a heavy sigh, Shaozhen hauled the rope back up, hand over fist. The empty bucket ricocheted and rattled against the sides of the well.

This wasn't the first time the well had gone dry. During the water shortage a few years back, all of the farmers had dug long channels to irrigate their fields from a nearby stream. Shaozhen remembered Ma being gone for hours to fetch water from the stream while he studied at home.

But both Headmaster Song and Nainai seemed to think that this drought was even worse. Could there really be no more water in the village?

Shaozhen squeezed his eyes shut, sending his wishes to the ancestors like Song had suggested. He gazed up at the bright white sky, the sun just embarking on its morning climb. He didn't know if the praying did any good, but it made him feel a little better. It was the very least he could do.

Five

Shaozhen traipsed through the narrow winding alleys and emerged at the entrance to the village. Straight ahead, a nearby mountain loomed over the concrete gate like a giant moon. As Shaozhen came to the well that the headmaster had mentioned, he recognised Chun, another boy about his age from the village. Like Shaozhen and Kang, Chun was an only child. Even though the country's one-child policy was less strict in villages than in the cities, most of the families in Hongsha just had the one.

Chun was crouched over the hole, hoisting the rope up. Shaozhen watched him peer inside, his expression grim. Shaozhen's heart sank.

'Chun. Any luck?'

'Hey, Shaozhen, no basketball today?' Chun said.

Shaozhen shook his head.

'How was school this year?' Unlike Shaozhen and Kang, Chun hadn't gone to middle school. Like Shaozhen's nainai, Chun's grandfather, Mongsok, felt strongly about his grandson learning to work in the fields. 'If he can't concentrate, what's the use? I'm perfectly fine and I didn't get past the third grade,' Mongsok had declared proudly to any of the villagers who would listen. Shaozhen's mother had tried to persuade Mongsok on the value of the boy's education but her pleas had fallen on deaf ears. Chun hadn't seemed to mind too much, but Shaozhen had always felt sorry for him.

'It was all right. I finished a couple of days ago. But Headmaster Song was saying I should try to get ahead for next year. Can you believe it? He's not even my teacher anymore.' He laughed nervously. Then he saw the blank stare from his friend and hastily changed the subject. 'So, no water?'

'Not a drop,' Chun said. 'I'm going to try the stream. There might be some water that hasn't been pumped or drained. You want to come?' He nodded to Shaozhen's buckets.

Shaozhen quickly agreed, relieved that someone was willing to point the way. The boys hefted the poles onto their backs and headed for the main road. They walked one behind the other in the direction of Xifeng. There were no cars travelling along the road, just the occasional farmer pedalling a bicycle or leading a niu.

Shaozhen noticed that Chun kept craning his neck towards the road anytime they heard the sputtering of an engine. 'You get that motorcycle of yours working yet?' he asked. Chun's uncle had moved to the city and left behind an old moped that Chun had been trying to fix.

'Nah. The engine's not turning over,' Chun said. 'I think I can try something with an old clock I found.'

Shaozhen had always thought his friend could have been an engineer or a mechanic if Mongsok hadn't pulled him out of school. He loved machines and tinkering with whatever broken gadgets and scrap parts he could find.

'Oh, that's a shame.' No one in the village had any transport except for bicycles and oxen for pulling carts; a motorcycle would certainly have made the rest of the summer more interesting.

'Yeah, maybe when the harvest is done I'll have time to really work on it.'

'Do you think we'll have an okay harvest?' Shaozhen couldn't help wondering aloud. Even though he didn't much care for the field work, Shaozhen was actually fond of harvest time. The villagers came together, even the small children, working on each other's fields one at a time until all the crops had been collected. Once the crops were sold and the money distributed, the villagers would cook up a huge, traditional water banquet feast to celebrate the Mid-Autumn Festival.

Chun was silent. He gave a little shrug. Shaozhen felt dread seeping through him, the same nauseating feeling he'd had when Ma left yesterday morning.

'Hey, maybe we should try a game of three-on-three this evening?' Shaozhen suggested hopefully. 'It's been a while.'

Chun laughed. 'I thought you'd gone into retirement. Didn't you say you wanted to give the rest of us a chance to win?'

'You wish you were that lucky! I can beat you carrying these buckets in one hand with the other tied behind my back!'

'Yeah, a game would be good,' Chun agreed. 'We could get Tingming and Wulei to come.'

Shaozhen tried to not to frown at the mention of Tingming. He was one of the oldest boys left in the village and considered himself their unofficial leader. He was a good basketball player but a bit of a bully; he gave Shaozhen a hard time, on and off the court. Shaozhen would have preferred not to have him along but he knew Tingming and Chun were good friends. Besides, the promise of a real game was much more important, so he said, 'Yeah. Maybe Kang will even play.'

Chun nodded and Shaozhen smiled. Playing basketball always made him feel better. 'Watch me take out most valuable player!' He leapt into the air, his buckets flopping around him like marooned fish.

'Wah! With you lot causing such a ruckus, it's no wonder we don't need scarecrows!' A short figure emerged from the plants, straw hat perched on her head.

'Aunty Law,' Shaozhen said, and Chun grinned. Law was a sturdy woman of about sixty. Her only daughter was working in the city and hadn't married, so Law wasn't looking after grandchildren the way so many of the other nainais and laobos in the village were.

Aunty Law came closer and waggled a finger at them. 'Wah, Shaozhen, I hope you're not avoiding your nainai like you were yesterday.'

Chun guffawed and Shaozhen chuckled nervously. There were no secrets in the village and everyone would have either seen or heard about Nainai pulling him by the ear.

Aunty Law pulled the straw hat off her head to fan her flushed face. Her hair was wild and stuck out at all angles, remnants of an ancient perm. 'This heat is killing us. And there isn't a cloud in sight. Just look, everything is drying up before our eyes.'

Shaozhen gazed out over her field and saw that her plants were in the same scorched, parched condition that Nainai's were, maybe even worse.

'It's okay… I'm sure it will rain soon.' Shaozhen knew he sounded feeble but he wasn't sure what else to say.

Aunty Law scoffed and spat at the ground. 'Hah, and I'm going to be young and beautiful again. Like Miss China, what do you think?' She struck a pose and batted her wrinkled eyelids like a model. Chun laughed again but Shaozhen felt awkward so he just readjusted his buckets on his shoulders.

'I'm just teasing, Shaozhen,' she said, swatting him with her hat. 'Are you always so serious?' She waved them away. 'Go, get your water. It won't be long before there's nothing left.'

Shaozhen kept staring at the crops – how pitiful they looked, swaying in the hot breeze. And when he couldn't bear to look anymore, they walked, and the rustling of the dry stalks seemed to gently mock him. The pair went on in silence, Shaozhen already feeling the weight of the buckets digging into his thin neck.

They followed the road until they came to a bridge that went over a small stream – or rather a bridge that *used* to go over a stream. Now, the concrete column rose up out of the parched ground. There was no water in sight.

Chun went off the path and descended the bank beside the bridge. Shaozhen followed with wobbly steps as he tried to balance the pole across his back. Only when they reached the bottom did Shaozhen spot the puddle of water underneath the bridge, barely protected from the sun. It was no more than a metre wide and a few centimetres deep; all that was left of the once swiftly flowing stream.

The earth beneath their feet was dry and cracked, more lines running through it than a sheet of bashed glass. Clumps of withered weeds were embedded between the cracks. It reminded Shaozhen of the pictures of the surface of the moon that he'd seen in his school textbooks – nothing but grey dust and jagged rocks – but even those images had looked more hospitable.

Shaozhen bit his bottom lip. He used to go fishing in this stream, dangling his line over the bridge hoping to catch something bigger than a minnow. The lifelessness of the scene before him pulled at something inside him. Could the village survive this? Shaozhen realised he was scared.

Chun approached the puddle, his buckets swaying. Shaozhen followed in stunned silence. Here, the earth was a bit softer, but hardly wet enough to be called mud.

They stopped by the puddle and Chun took one of his buckets and tilted it on its side. Shaozhen frowned as Chun scraped the rim along the ground, picking up something that resembled mud more than water. The greyish flecks spinning through the water made it look revolting. How would they ever get it clear?

The boys collected as much liquid as they could. They found a few more decent-sized puddles further upstream. At one point, they found a ribbon of water that twisted along the ground like a sick eel. They kept going, picking up a scoop of water here and another from there, using an empty bucket to fill the others. Their other buckets grew heavier and heavier until they were almost full. Shaozhen's shoulders ached from the weight. He was glad he hadn't brought the other pole.

They were turning to leave the last puddle, a sizeable one about a li, half a kilometre, from the bridge, when an old woman approached. She wasn't familiar to them, so she must have come from one of the nearby villages. She didn't say a word, just plonked her buckets onto the ground, then reached into her shirt and pulled out a plastic bottle.

'Ah, Po, Grandmother, you can't drink the water,' Shaozhen said matter-of-factly as she plunged her bottle into the murky liquid. It squelched and bubbled as it sucked up the sludge.

'Little boy, you think at sixty-nine-years old I don't know the difference between drinkable and non-drinkable water?' She looked up at him, narrowing her small round eyes and pulling her wormlike lips together.

She pulled the bottle out of the sludge and reached into her shirt again. 'Some tricks you learn with old age.' She held up a teeny sachet and gave the boys a wink. 'Watch this.'

The boys went over to her, curious as to what the old lady would do. She tore off the corner of the sachet and dumped its contents into the greyish water. Then she shook the bottle furiously so that the water spiralled around like a cyclone.

Eventually the swirling stopped and the old woman let out a cackle. The boys stepped closer. 'Patience,' she said.

They waited. At first Shaozhen thought he was imagining it but then he saw the water become clearer, the muddy sediment coming together and settling at the bottom.

He stepped back in surprise. The old woman pulled her lips apart to reveal a single dingy brown tooth. 'What'd I tell you?' She unscrewed the cap and drank. Shaozhen made a face. The water *was* clearer but it still looked disgusting.

'No, thank you,' they both said politely when the woman offered them a sip. She shrugged, tucked the bottle into her shirt and hummed to herself as she filled her buckets. The boys retrieved their water haul, careful not to spill a drop.

Six

The buckets rocked wildly as Shaozhen trudged unsteadily up the bank to the bridge. The walk home was excruciating. With the weight digging into his neck, and his hands clutching the bamboo rods to keep the buckets from sliding off, Shaozhen felt like an awkward, lumbering tree. It took all his focus just to put one foot in front of the other. Chun didn't falter, clearly used to the task. His muscles were taut and his footsteps solid.

The rumbling of an engine drew the boys' attention. Motor vehicles were still rare around these parts. As far has Shaozhen knew, only the former Village Secretary had ever owned a car. Secretary Fan Luqiao once had a flashy luxury sedan that he claimed was given to him for 'Party business'. It was later discovered he had siphoned the money to pay for the car directly from the village coffers. He had recently been dismissed from his post for corruption. He lost all respect among the villagers and they only ever referred to him by his first name rather than his official title.

'I wonder who that could be?' Shaozhen said.

Chun whistled low and steady as his gaze followed the car down the road. The vehicle was definitely second-hand but well-cared-for, with shiny chrome and a fresh coat of paint. It had an official look about it, although it was more stately than showy.

'Looks like Secretary Lam's car,' Chun concluded. 'An Audi 100 C3 sedan. Ninety-six, I reckon. Saw it parked outside the Party headquarters in Xifeng,' he said with pride. Chun knew a lot about engines and cars.

'Why would the Town Secretary come to Hongsha?' Shaozhen wondered out loud. The Town Secretary was one rank above the Village Secretary and was in charge of the various village communities within the township.

'Maybe we're getting a new Luqiao?' Chun suggested. 'It's been a couple of months now.'

'Do we want a new Luqiao?' Shaozhen replied.

The former Village Secretary had been a rather proud-looking man with a perm and pot belly. He'd spent a lot of time strolling through the village with an air of grandiose authority. He liked to chew on roasted pumpkin seeds, cracking the shells between his teeth and then spitting them all over the road.

One time a few of the boys had been playing on the court. Shaozhen had just driven the ball past a monstrous defence mounted by Chun and Tingming. When Tingming had shot up for the rebound, they'd heard a slow clapping from the sidelines, where they discovered the Village Secretary observing their game.

'A fine example of teamwork and discipline from our future Party members. Hongsha has its own Young Pioneers!' Luqiao had declared, his cheeks pulled back into an eerie smile. He gave them a funny little wave, two fingers tucked into his palm, his gold rings catching the light. The next evening when they went to the court, Luqiao was waiting for them, dressed in bright white basketball shorts with a whistle hanging around his neck. A cheap portable stereo was sitting on the picnic table. When he pressed play, a revolutionary song blasted through the tinny speakers. 'All right, boys, you can call me Coach.'

The boys had stopped going to the court after that, even Shaozhen, who lived and breathed the game. Instead he practised at home. The boys had been quite relieved when Luqiao had been dismissed from his position.

Outside their strange encounter on the basketball court, he and the rest of the boys had steered clear of political figures and village affairs, all that 'old people stuff'. He wasn't sure now how he felt about getting a new Village Secretary.

As they walked closer to the centre of the village, they saw that the car had parked outside the village headquarters. The headquarters were another legacy of Luqiao's extravagance; the pragmatic two-storey concrete building had been renovated at vast expense, including the addition of a grand entrance with gilded iron gates, complete with a pair of marble lion statues.

A small crowd was gathered at the gates. Some of the villagers had even come in from the fields when they had noticed the vehicle arriving. Shaozhen and Chun set down their buckets and hurried over.

The vehicle was empty but the engine was still running. The boys squeezed past the villagers until they were at the front of the gates and had an unobstructed view of the courtyard beyond.

Shaozhen immediately recognised the wiry man with silver hair. Secretary Lam was known for taking extra care with his appearance: his clothes were crisp and his leather shoes, though worn, were always buffed to a shine.

More curious was the younger man standing next to him, dressed in crumpled slacks and a creased, untucked shirt. He certainly hadn't taken the same time getting ready for this meeting that Secretary Lam had. Shaozhen could see his face clearly. It was youthful, which made Shaozhen think he couldn't really be that much older than he and Chun were.

The doors to the headquarters opened and Headmaster Song strolled out. Shaozhen pressed his face against the bars, trying to make out what they were saying. With the chatter from the other villagers surrounding him, he had to strain his ears to catch more than just snippets of the conversation.

'Mr Song, how are you?' Secretary Lam sounded friendly but restrained as Song approached him. 'I see Hongsha is faring rather well despite the misfortunes of Mr Fan Luqiao.'

'I'd hardly say that we are faring well, Secretary Lam,' Song said. 'As I've mentioned to you countless times, we have no crops to harvest and many of our residents are struggling to find enough water for their daily needs.'

Lam appeared uneasy, clasping his hands together and forcing a bright smile. 'The drought. Well, it seems like you're making do. The province is suffering and we are all doing our part. And I'm sure you will be pleased that I've taken the time and attention to look after you myself, Mr Song. Don't think that Hongsha hasn't been on my radar.' He rocked forwards onto the toes of his leather shoes. 'In fact, that is exactly why I am here,' he said quickly, gesturing to the young man beside him. 'Mr Song, I want to introduce you to Mr Xian Zuluan. He is one of the top graduates from Chengdu University, top ten per cent of your class – isn't that right?'

'Twenty-five per cent, sir,' Xian stammered.

Lam's expression flickered in surprise. 'Well, there you go. Twenty-five per cent is certainly nothing to sneer at.' He leant forwards so that he was hovering over Song. 'Xian is going to be the new Village Secretary. And as the head of the village committee, Mr Song, I thought you could make him feel welcome.'

Shaozhen was stunned. Village Secretary? But Xian was practically a boy! And it showed. The young Xian was visibly nervous, his eyes darting about as the villagers watched him. His button-down shirt looked too big, his shoulders too narrow, his limbs long and awkward like a toy puppet's. How was he going to help the village? How would he solve their water problem?

Xian crossed his arms and cast his gaze downwards.

If Headmaster Song was surprised by the introduction, he didn't seem to show it. Instead, he offered a hand to the boy. 'Of course, we are delighted to have you, Secretary Xian.' He had on his headmaster's voice, the one he used when the boys in his charge were misbehaving. 'Perhaps we should all come in and have a cup of tea, acquaint ourselves with each other.' He motioned towards the headquarters before them.

'I think that's an excellent suggestion, Song. But I'll have to leave Xian with you as I have to return to my duties at Xifeng.' Secretary Lam said this a bit too loudly, with an air of importance. The younger Secretary looked alarmed while the headmaster just nodded.

'Shall we?' Song motioned to Xian. The pair headed inside and shut the door without so much as a glance towards the crowd at the front. Party matters were not for the public eye.

Secretary Lam returned to his vehicle while two guards inside rushed to open the gates, shooing the villagers aside. The car rumbled slowly down the gravel road towards the village entrance.

The villagers refrained from commenting until the roar of the engine was out of earshot. Then the chattering began.

'The new Luqiao? Are they joking?'

'He's still sucking from his ma's teats!' one old man exclaimed crudely.

'He's a child. He'll be too scared to take bribes.'

'How is he going to help us old folks?'

'Top of his class indeed! Did you see how pale he looked? I don't think he's been out in the sun for an entire day in all his life!'

And on it went.

'What do you think, Chun?' Shaozhen asked. 'A new Secretary could be good.'

His friend shrugged. 'As long as he's not another Luqiao.' He picked up his buckets. 'I should go tell my grandfather we have a new Secretary. I wonder what he'll think. He's never been a fan of the politics,' Chun mused.

The boys went their separate ways. As he walked, Shaozhen found himself intrigued by the new Village Secretary. He wasn't an old, stubborn farmer like so many of the elderly villagers including Nainai, Mongsok or Lao Zhu. His simple clothes and nervous demeanour meant he wasn't likely to squander funds for his own personal gain, like Luqiao had. Maybe, just maybe, Xian really could make things better.

●●●

Shaozhen hurried home as fast as he could, straining under the weight of his water buckets. He was bursting to tell everyone the news. Nainai was still out working in the fields but Yangyang was in the kitchen, brushing dirt from a freshly picked cabbage.

'Wah, you've been gone all morning and only managed two buckets of water?' Yangyang wasted no time reproaching him.

Shaozhen rolled his eyes as he pulled back the lid of

the tank they were using to store water. 'Not now. Did you hear? We have a new Village Secretary! He's from the city.' He was about to empty the liquid from his buckets into the container but Yangyang snatched them away.

'Do you know nothing? You have to filter out the particles first.' She laid a muslin cloth over the top of the tank, tying down the corners to form a loose drum. Then she carefully poured the water onto the cloth, letting it slowly drain into the container. The mud and sediment gathered on top of the fabric. Shaozhen felt a bit sick remembering the old woman drinking her weird bottle of sludge.

'I hope this new Secretary can help us,' she mused. 'The village is in big trouble if we don't have a decent harvest in eight weeks. Where did you say he was from?'

'He went to Chengdu University. Graduated top of his class.'

Yangyang narrowed her eyes. 'From the city? How's a city boy going to help our village?'

'You're so judgemental. I think it's good to have someone with a more modern viewpoint here. Hongsha is so boring.'

'You only get bored if you're lazy. You should be more like Tingming. He works hard on his grandfather's farm. He's an adult, not a boy.'

Shaozhen rolled his eyes again. With his broad forehead and squinty eyes, Tingming looked more like a monkey than a man, but for some reason Yangyang was infatuated with the older boy. Her usual snark and sharp tongue melted into smiles and giggles when

Tingming was around, to the point where Shaozhen felt like puking.

It was still amusing to poke fun at Yangyang though. 'Wah, with your horse laugh you think Tingming would take a second look at you?'

To Shaozhen's surprise, her face went red. She almost never reacted to his comments and he felt a wave of satisfaction about finally getting under her skin. He was about to add more when they heard Nainai coming up to the house. There were sounds of scraping as she leant her tools against the doorway and then came inside. She stared at Yangyang and Shaozhen pouring the water.

'Just two buckets? I thought I told you to take both poles!'

Shaozhen flinched, automatically expecting her to reach for his lobes again, but she didn't. Instead, she took the basin of brushed vegetables that Yangyang had prepared, went to another container and pried off the lid. Inside was water that had previously been used for washing vegetables and recollected. With water so scarce, they were reusing whatever they could. She scooped a few precious ladles into the basin and began to scrub the leaves of the cabbage.

'Did you hear the news, Nainai? There's a new Village Secretary. His name is Xian. He has to do a better job than that old Luqiao, eh?' Shaozhen knew Nainai had always despised Luqiao – mentioning him was an easy way to get her mind off the missing buckets of water.

'New Village Secretary? What's he going to do?' she scoffed, her eyes scanning the leaves of the cabbage, looking for insects. 'All these new Party folk do is try to figure out how to help themselves in Beijing, and how to take us old folks for everything we're worth.'

'He can make things better,' Shaozhen said. 'Build more infrastructure, make things modern, like in the cities.'

'Can he make it rain?' she spat. 'You lot think your life is so difficult now. If only you knew.'

Shaozhen sighed. He was not surprised by Nainai's cynicism. In school, they were taught about the Party's new policies and visions for a better China, and he believed them. Development and modernisation would mean a better life and more local opportunity. More local opportunity meant his parents wouldn't have to go all the way to the city to find jobs.

But Nainai and the other elderly folks didn't seem to believe in these ideas. They were more focused on protecting the land.

Nainai was muttering, as if reading to his mind, 'The only thing I want is to be buried alongside my ancestors on our family plot. Leave me there in peace, and I'll be happy.'

Shaozhen knew better than to say anything. Whenever he asked questions about politics or why she was so suspicious of the Party's intentions, she always gave vague answers that trailed off to nothing.

'Shaozhen, go take some of the washing water to the pigs,' Nainai barked, breaking into his thoughts.

She emptied the water she had just used for washing the vegies into a bowl. 'Not too much though, or there won't be any left for us.'

Shaozhen frowned but went to the back of the house. He watched the thirsty pigs drink while his mind swam with questions.

Seven

Shaozhen was finally free of his chores late in the evening. Nainai had worked him to the bone, but the boys had promised to play basketball and he wasn't going to miss out.

Chun was already on the court when he arrived, along with his cousin, Bo. There was another village boy called Wulei, as well as Tingming. Kang had come too, though he only ever watched from the sidelines.

'Shaozhen, wah! I almost didn't recognise you with that farmer's stoop!' Tingming called out as Shaozhen approached the court. 'You're becoming a regular peasant boy.'

Everyone laughed. Shaozhen bristled, trying to come up with a retort, but he had never been good at thinking on his feet. Instead he chucked the basketball at the older boy with force. But Tingming was ready and snatched the ball smoothly out of the air with one hand. The boys *oohed*, clearly impressed. Even Shaozhen had to begrudgingly admit that Tingming had skills.

'Where's Zhanfu?' Shaozhen asked.

'Didn't you hear? His papers came through. He's gone to Zhengzhou,' said Wulei.

'Really? He's gone to the city?' Shaozhen was surprised. Zhanfu had only turned sixteen about a month ago, and wasn't even one of the oldest boys in the village.

For village boys like themselves, going to the city was the dream. There was no real future for them if they stayed in Hongsha, aside from getting married, having kids and then leaving them behind just like their parents had left them. Many of the youths wanted to go to Zhengzhou, Guangzhou or Beijing and join their parents, but getting the right permits was hard. They had to wait until they were at least sixteen and could apply to be migrant workers.

'Yeah, he left yesterday,' Tingming said. Shaozhen couldn't help noticing the bitterness in his voice. He knew Tingming had been hoping for city work for months but the only way to secure a position without already being in the city was by recommendation. 'His dad found him a job at a new shoe factory. Says they need more young workers. So' – Tingming puffed out his chest – 'he's going to try to get me a job too. He could probably find something for all of us, well, us older ones anyway.' He nodded deliberately at Chun, Bo and Wulei.

Shaozhen felt a surprising pang of jealousy shoot through him. He wasn't itching to work in a shoe factory but he didn't like Tingming excluding him and Kang. He glowered at the older boy, who returned a lazy smile.

'So are we going to play ball or what?' Shaozhen said loudly. He put his hands on his hips and scanned the group. 'With Zhanfu gone, you're going to have to play, Kang.'

'Nah, I – I'll just keep score or something.' Kang never liked playing sports.

'Come on. If you don't play, we won't have enough people for two teams.' The other boys nodded. Kang's eyes grew to the size of dishes behind his glasses.

'Good evening, young comrades,' a bold voice called out from the road.

The boys swivelled their heads in surprise. The young Secretary was standing at the edge of the court, a basketball tucked under his arm.

'Mind if I join you?'

Secretary Xian stepped onto the court. Shaozhen felt his pulse quickening and his mind flashed back to the strange revolutionary coaching session with Luqiao. But Xian didn't look like he was trying to push an agenda. If anything, Shaozhen thought he looked a bit uneasy.

Xian's youthful features were perfectly smooth, like the pictures of the famous actors that featured in the billboards on the freeway. But his teeth were too wide, his nose too broad and his forehead too squat for him to ever be mistaken for a model.

'Friends.' He smiled broadly and scanned the group, his eyes landing on Tingming. 'I'm Xian. I'm from Zhengzhou, but my grandfather came from Xiaosong.'

Xiaosong was an old remote village, now just a cluster of houses a treacherous thirty-minute hike up

55

the mountainside. Shaozhen was surprised. He hadn't considered that Xian could have local roots – he certainly didn't sound or look like he did.

Tingming shook the Secretary's hand gruffly.

Shaozhen stepped forwards. 'Nice to meet you. I'm Shaozhen and this is Chun, Bo, Kang, Tingming and Wulei.' He introduced the boys in turn. 'Welcome to Hongsha.'

The Secretary beamed, the brightness of his smile punctuating his unblemished face. Tingming scoffed but Shaozhen couldn't help but puff with pride.

'Nice to be here. You boys like to play basketball?'

'Except for Kang. He prefers reading, so he just watches,' Shaozhen explained.

Kang turned crimson, and hunched his shoulders around his ears like he was trying to slip into a shell.

But Xian smiled. 'That's great. I think I'm more of a books boy myself, but I don't mind a game every now and then.' He balanced the ball on the tip of his fingers as he said this. He didn't have the flair of an NBA pro, but it was still impressive. With a smirk, he flicked a pass to Shaozhen. 'So how about a game of three-on-three?' he said.

The boys looked from one to the other and they all nodded in agreement. Shaozhen was relieved that they could finally play some *real* basketball.

They split up into teams: Secretary Xian, Tingming and Wulei on one side; Shaozhen, Chun and Bo on the other. Xian's team took the ball out first. Shaozhen was impressed. Xian moved fast and wasn't intimidated by his outsider status. He found an opening and fired the ball to Wulei, who completed the play with an easy lay-up and two points.

Shaozhen snatched the rebound and squared off against Tingming. The burly teen tried to use his size to block him, but Shaozhen got away with a sidestep left, a faked right. He came around the other side and shot a bounce pass to Chun, who took it to the basket.

Two points.

The play continued this way for a while, both teams evenly matched in ability and skill. Sweat clung to their backs. Tingming stripped down to his undershirt, his broad shoulders and bulging muscles on display.

The score was tied. Shaozhen had the ball. He dribbled carefully, keeping his eyes trained on Tingming, who was moving into position to guard him. Shaozhen felt Tingming's penetrating gaze focused on his every move. He swivelled left and right, but Tingming stayed with him, a brutal barrier closing in.

Feeling boxed out, Shaozhen decided to try and make a break for it. He twisted down and under, imagining he was an eel snaking his way through watery muck, trusting his instincts to push him towards the basket. Tingming was like an octopus, limbs everywhere. There was no way out and in a move of sheer desperation – a 'Hail Mary' as the Americans called it – Shaozhen lunged blindly up and forwards. He felt the ball leaving his fingertips on the wings of hope, but at the last moment, Tingming's forearm sliced through the air and knocked his hand away.

The ball sailed up and over the basket and ricocheted off the top of the backboard, before shattering the window of the village primary school.

Shaozhen gasped. He clapped his hand over his mouth, staring at the jagged hole in the pane of glass. He could still hear the ball bouncing to a stop within the room.

Tingming ambled over to inspect the damage and let out a low whistle. 'Yikes. Shaozhen, do we need to show you what the basket looks like?'

Shaozhen clenched his fists by his side, fuming. 'You fouled me. I couldn't see a thing. I didn't mean to—'

The sound of Xian's slow clapping interrupted him. He clasped his hands together above his head. 'Wow. Great game, boys! I haven't seen that much excitement in a while.' He pointed to Tingming and Shaozhen. 'You two have the skills to rival any player on a university team.'

Tingming bowed humbly. 'Secretary, thank you for your praise. I'm just sorry my friend here broke your window.'

'You *fouled* me!' Shaozhen protested, furious with himself as much as he was with Tingming.

But the Secretary waved it off. 'It's okay. These things happen. The school is due for maintenance over the summer anyway.' He smiled. 'I'm sure the Party can manage that.'

Shaozhen's shoulders sagged with relief. There was no way his family had the money to pay for a new window for the school.

Tingming frowned but he didn't say any more. The game was over, ending on a tie. Secretary Xian let Shaozhen into the school to retrieve his basketball. The boys high-fived each other and went their separate ways.

Shaozhen was still checking for bits of glass on his basketball when Xian called out to him. 'Shaozhen, how about we have a quick cup of tea at my house?' Xian suggested.

Shaozhen was surprised, wondering if the Secretary had changed his mind about him paying for the window. But Xian was smiling, his eyes warm and friendly. 'S-sure, I don't think Nainai would mind if I'm a little late,' he stammered.

Xian was already set up in Luqiao's old residence, a large three-storey house standing alone at the edge of the village. Luqiao had wasted no time building the spectacular residence during his abbreviated term. The house had a walled courtyard with a circle-shaped entrance, a traditional moon gate. But the rest of the house was more modern – all concrete, metal and chrome – though Shaozhen thought it was a little garish. The slick roof was made of shiny black tiles and large glass panels covered windows cut out of the gleaming white walls. A battered old truck was parked outside the front.

Shaozhen paused in the courtyard, gaping up at his reflection on the mirrored doors that served as the entrance. 'Are you living here alone?'

Xian swallowed. 'Yeah, I'm not married. Well, not yet.' He gave a sheepish smile and bounded up the steps. 'Please, come inside.'

Shaozhen followed wordlessly, in awe of the grandiose building.

'It's a bit much for me,' Xian said apologetically. 'To be honest, I would have preferred something simpler, but the Town Secretary said there was no point in wastage.' He gave a little shrug. 'I'm used to a crowded college dormitory.'

The opulence was apparent on the interior as well. The floor was polished concrete, so unlike the bare earth of the typical village home. Instead of a single all-purpose family room, this house had a separate space for cooking at the front with a large window that overlooked the courtyard. There was an elegant round table with matching chairs, made from hardwood stained dark like the midnight sky and then lacquered to a lustrous shine. Here, there were no folding chairs and wobbly tables that had to be stowed away after each meal. No random boxes of appliances stacked on top of each other in the middle of the room. And the lightbulbs overhead had shades, so that when Xian flicked the switch, a soft light cascaded gently through the room without blinding anyone.

Shaozhen walked into the centre of the room, careful not to touch anything. On the rare times he had come to the premises, Luqiao had never invited him or any of the other villagers inside, not even Headmaster Song. Only the more senior Party members, such as Secretary Lam, were ever welcomed inside the home.

Something caught Shaozhen's eye. 'Wah, look at the TV! It has a flat screen!' They had a small colour TV at home, but he had never seen one this big or new before. He rushed over and peered at the sides, looking for the buttons to press.

'Here.' Xian picked up a black box wrapped in clear crumpled plastic and waved it through the air. Like magic, the screen flickered to life showing a female reporter delivering the late evening news.

Shaozhen put his face right up to the screen. 'Wah! That's so clear. Look – you can even see her mole!'

'The reception's not very good here, so the picture still goes in and out,' Xian said as he muted the sound. 'In the city it's much better.'

'Wah! You have a computer too!' Shaozhen marvelled at the two screens, a colourful joystick and the set of speakers sitting on the worn desk in the corner. He had only ever used a computer at school where the network coverage was good enough for wi-fi. While some of the villagers had mobile phones, they rarely used them since the signal in Hongsha was unreliable. Even fewer residents had home phones; the village simply didn't have the infrastructure to connect more homes.

'Satellite internet. But it's pretty expensive so I can't imagine that I would use it very often. Please have a seat.' He motioned towards an oversized leather chair facing two rather plain-looking wicker stools.

Shaozhen sat down gingerly, but he was immediately pulled into the chair's cushioning comfort. It felt like he had fallen into a giant cloud, his neck cool against the pillowy headrest. He peered over the side and saw a small lever. Xian smiled and motioned for Shaozhen to pull on it. He did, and the chair moved back and a footrest rose out from the bottom, propping up his feet. 'Ah! So comfy.' Shaozhen couldn't help giggling.

Xian smiled. 'I'll go make some tea.' He moved towards the kitchen. Shaozhen felt awkward sitting by himself in the grand room, so he rose and followed Xian.

'You were in Chengdu?' Shaozhen asked as he leant against the doorway.

'At the university. Not one of the best schools, but I'm just glad I had the marks to get in.'

Shaozhen stared as Xian pulled out an oversized bottle of water, the expensive kind that he saw vendors selling in town sometimes. The Secretary broke the seal on the lid and hoisted the bottle onto the stove.

'What's living in the city like?' Shaozhen asked.

'Chengdu is nice,' Xian said, as he poured some of the water into an electric jug. 'I like it more than I liked growing up in Wuhan. The air quality is a bit better.' He replaced the cap, checking it to make sure it was screwed tight, and returned the water to the cupboard. He turned back to Shaozhen as he flicked the switch on the jug for the water to boil.

'Oh really? That's good.' Shaozhen smiled quickly, ashamed to have been caught staring. *Being the Village Secretary definitely has its perks, even when it comes to water.*

'The house and the stuff – none of it's mine.' Xian toed the edge of the cupboard. 'My parents gave me the bottles of water,' he admitted sheepishly. 'Everyone in Wuhan is hoarding them because of the drought.'

Shaozhen was surprised. 'The drought has affected Wuhan too?'

Xian nodded. 'All of Henan, Hubei, Shandong and beyond is dry. There's no water coming from the taps and the reservoirs are empty. Everyone is using bottled water.' He eyed the jug, pulling his lower lip under his teeth. 'The drought issue is of utmost importance and a priority issue for the Party,' he said finally. Those words were firm but stilted in delivery and Shaozhen wondered whether they had been fed to Xian by someone higher up, like Secretary Lam.

Tinkling music came from the electric jug, a tune from a child's nursery rhyme. Xian put a teapot with loose leaves under the jug and pressed the round knob at the top. Steaming water spurted into the teapot with each press.

'I want to make some serious changes here, Shaozhen,' Xian said unexpectedly. 'The village is in dire condition and requires lots of work beyond just the primary school. Headmaster Song is admired and well-respected, but he's afraid to ruffle feathers. He wants to do things the old-fashioned way. But if we stick to traditions, China will never modernise. Don't you agree?'

'I – I guess so,' Shaozhen stammered. Xian might have looked like a regular teen boy, but he was worldly. He had big ideas about things that Shaozhen knew nothing about.

The Secretary looked pleased with his reply. He swirled the pot then poured some tea into two cups, their rims edged with brass, not chipped or cracked like the ones in Shaozhen's home. The tea was light and fragrant, earthy and reassuring.

Xian handed him a cup, gripping it at the lip so as not to burn his fingers. Shaozhen held his cup in the same way. 'I want to help the residents of Hongsha achieve a better future for themselves. That means taking care of the drought situation, and more. Will you help me in my mission, Shaozhen?' Xian raised his cup, ready for a toast.

Shaozhen nodded solemnly. Xian broke into a wide grin as the pair clinked their cups together and sipped at their tea.

The moon was almost at its highest point when Shaozhen finally left the Secretary's house. The air felt cooler but it was still uncomfortably hot for this time of night. Shaozhen hardly noticed. His mind was buzzing, the hot tea warming his stomach. Tomorrow he'd have to face another hard day's work in the fields. Tomorrow his mother would still be in the city, and tomorrow there still wouldn't be any water in the wells. But after his evening with Xian, hearing the new Secretary's glistening promises, he couldn't help but feel hopeful.

Eight

'Get up, sleeping pig!'

Shaozhen awoke with a start. His bleary eyes finally registered that something was flying through the air, aimed at his head.

'Hey, watch it!' he cried as the wicker basket bounced off his half-sitting form and clattered to the floor. 'You'll take someone's eye out.'

'Get up, layabout,' Yangyang huffed. 'The birds have already been awake for an hour.'

'I'm not a bird,' Shaozhen grumbled under his breath as he slung his feet over the side of the bed. He didn't bother lighting the gas lamp in his room, and found his sandals in the dark, slipping them on while fumbling for a shirt. 'What's that for?' He eyed the basket.

'I weaved that with my own hands. No poles and buckets where we're headed. Now come on, hurry up. Get dressed. We need to get going.'

'Is Nainai even awake yet? It's too early for field work.'

Yangyang groaned with exasperation. 'Don't you get it, bendan, fool? There's no point doing any more farm work, because there's no *water*.'

Shaozhen blinked in the darkness, letting her words sink in. 'No water?' he whispered finally.

'Not a drop.'

The sky was just beginning to lighten when they emerged from the house. Yangyang had made wicker baskets for them both, the insides lined with plastic so they would stay watertight. They had slung them over their shoulders and secured them to their backs with thick twine straps, like they were backpacks. Yangyang hooked her thumbs beneath the straps, her back arched, head tilted high with steely determination. Meanwhile, Shaozhen dragged himself along behind her.

The birds tweeted, their songs somehow harmonising with the crunch of sand and gravel beneath Shaozhen's feet.

'Shaozhen. Yangyang.' The voice came from behind. They turned towards the sound of footsteps hurrying to catch up with them.

'Kang, what are you doing?' Yangyang hissed. 'You can't come with us.'

'Why? Where are you going?' Kang's eyes lit up.

'Who died and made you the empress?' Shaozhen scowled and turned to his best friend. 'We're going to get water. You can come if you want.'

'He's just going to slow us down. Besides, I don't have another basket.'

Shaozhen frowned, unsure of what else to say.

'I – I can bring a bucket,' Kang suggested.

'See, he can bring a bucket!' Shaozhen beamed at his friend's cleverness. 'Hurry up. Go get it and you can come with us.'

They watched him scamper off. He returned minutes later, a large plastic bucket in tow. It was almost as tall as his torso.

Yangyang rolled her eyes. 'A lot of use that's going to be.'

'Oh come on, lighten up,' Shaozhen said. 'I say he comes or none of us go.'

'Whatever.' Yangyang rolled her eyes again. 'Come on, four eyes, you'd better not fall behind.'

Kang looked as though he was about to say something but then thought better of it and clamped his mouth shut. Shaozhen gave his friend a wink to try to lighten the mood. He was quite relieved to have Kang's company; he wasn't sure he could deal with Yangyang's venomous nature all by himself.

The road to the mountains took them away from the township and deeper into the Henan countryside. They went past many fields, all with shrivelled and shrunken crops. About a li along, the path divided and they followed the narrower left fork into the woods, which led them to a set of rickety wooden stairs. The sun had risen now, the intense rays beating down on them as they climbed. The mountain loomed above, brown, grey and lifeless, like the great Buddha had stuck a straw in and sucked it dry.

Shaozhen used to enjoy hiking with his father when he was little. He delighted in the scent of the air and its crisp coolness against the skin, like a cloud's breath. He loved peering up through the treetops, watching the bolts of sunlight dancing between the leaves like shimmering gold. His father had taught him to listen for signs of wildlife hidden among the canopy.

The elder Lu used to keep a pair of small birds, grey warblers, in a handsome handmade bamboo cage. Each morning, he took the birds in their cage up to the mountains. 'This way they can see from up high, like they were flying,' his father explained.

'But if you let them out, they could really fly,' the young Shaozhen had reasoned. His father had laughed and stroked him on the head. But he'd kept the birds caged and continued to take them up the mountain.

On the day after his father had left for Guangzhou, Shaozhen had taken the birds up the mountain one last time. He had opened the door and let them free.

Shaozhen shook his head to release the stinging from his eyes. He was missing Ma and Ba. The heat and the drought, the harshness of the mountain climb and the dryness of his surrounds were taking their toll on him.

'Get a move on,' Yangyang snapped, interrupting his thoughts. She had led them deeper into the woods, but he didn't feel the usual coolness of the mountain air enveloping him. Instead, the air was dry and the tops of the trees were too thin to provide much shade. The forest floor was littered with dry leaves and ready-made kindling.

The trio reached the top of the stairs and had to continue the climb up the mountain unaided. Yangyang was surefooted, hopping across the rocks without hesitation, her thumbs still hooked into the straps of the basket at her back. Shaozhen followed behind, using his hands to steady himself as he tried to match her steps. Kang brought up the rear, struggling to keep up. It soon became clear why Yangyang had deemed the bucket a hindrance, as it flailed around him like an unwieldy fifth limb.

Kang and Shaozhen were panting from the effort of the climb. They came to a small clearing and took a brief rest, despite Yangyang's protests. Shaozhen wiped the sweat from his brow and arched his aching back.

'Hey, what's that?' he asked, pointing up the embankment. A small rocky path led upwards to a rundown shack built into the side of the mountain. 'I didn't know there were cave people here.'

'It's not a cave, it's a house,' Yangyang replied.

Curious, Shaozhen followed the path for a few metres. It was slightly overgrown, but the trampled weeds told Shaozhen it was still in use. 'I didn't know anyone lived up this way.' But the dwelling seemed abandoned, no tell-tale smoke or signs of residence that he could see from his position. He went a little further along the path. Nainai had told him that the mountains used to be full of houses but the inhabitants had all moved down to the valleys and villages a long time ago. Yet there were still stories of Shaolin monks and hidden temples tucked into the corners, a secret from society.

'Shaozhen! Come on, you're wasting time!' Yangyang shouted. 'We need to get water, not muck around looking at old houses.'

Shaozhen cast one more look at the ragtag dwelling before hurrying back down the path to re-join the pair.

They continued climbing. Sweat clung to Shaozhen's back and the basket felt like a ton of bricks. His mouth was parched and he longed for a sip of water. He could hear the *thunk thunk thunk* of Kang's bucket slamming against the cliff face as they climbed.

Eventually the path levelled out and they could walk in a steady line. But moving forwards was no easier. The cliff face was narrow and they had to cling to the wall as they inched along. At one point, Shaozhen peered over the side and immediately regretted it. It was at least an 800-metre drop into the pointy branches of the barren trees. He sucked in a deep breath and tried not to think about going over. Instead, he focused on the path ahead.

'We had better not be carrying him back,' Yangyang grumbled, peering over Shaozhen's shoulder to Kang. Shaozhen pivoted his head just enough to see what she was whining about.

Kang was plastered against the cliff wall, his left hand shaking as it clutched the handle of the bucket. His glasses were practically falling off his nose and Shaozhen could see he was biting his lip to keep himself from crying.

'Kang, it's okay,' he called. He made his way back to his terrified friend. 'Take my hand, come on.'

Kang's fingers felt clammy as they closed around his.

'Deep breaths. It's going to be fine.' Shaozhen hoped his voice sounded reassuring. He reached out and took Kang's bucket.

Shaozhen turned back to the cliff edge and focused on placing one foot in front of the other. Kang gripped his hand so tightly he started to lose feeling in it, but Shaozhen didn't let go. Eventually, they turned a corner and the path widened. They were back among the trees again. The cover was thicker on this side of the mountain, the leaves greener, and the air deliciously cool. It felt much more like the mountains that he remembered from the days of hiking with his father.

'Almost there.' Yangyang's face was grim, but Shaozhen could see a bubble of excitement in her eyes.

'About time,' Shaozhen replied.

They walked down a gentle slope and came to another cliff face. Shaozhen heard Kang stifling a whimper.

But instead of going down the narrow ledge, Yangyang veered left so suddenly that Shaozhen nearly didn't see her turn. The boys followed and saw what they would have missed: Yangyang had led them to the mouth of a small cave.

'Come on.' Yangyang dropped onto all fours and crawled in through the tight entrance. Shaozhen and Kang did the same.

The opening was small but once they were past it, the cavern opened out and they could stand up. It took a while for Shaozhen's eyes to adjust to the darkness, with the only light coming from the mouth of the cave. He listened to Yangyang moving about and then he registered something else: a gentle babbling.

It was the sound of trickling water. He felt his heart leap upwards and into his mouth.

'A spring,' Kang said, full of awe. 'How did you find it, Yangyang?'

'What do you think we did in Sichuan?' she scoffed. 'Henan isn't the only province to have a drought, you know. I was the best at finding water back home. We all would have died if it weren't for my cunning.'

Usually, Shaozhen would have found himself annoyed by Yangyang's boasting, but right now he was exceptionally impressed.

Yangyang knelt beside a pool of water. 'The mountains are the best source of clean, fresh water. You just have to know where to look.' She took a long, loud slurp.

Shaozhen dipped a hand into the water. It was warm, and the pool was shallower than he had first thought, but even in the dim light, he could tell the water was crystal clear. He cupped his palm, brought his hand to his lips and took a sip.

Maybe it was the long walk they'd taken or maybe it was the rancid water he'd become used to drinking from the village stream, but Shaozhen was sure he had never tasted anything so amazing.

'Come on, we've wasted enough time.' Yangyang was opening her basket. 'If we hurry back, we can make one more trip before it's too dark.'

They filled their baskets up and Yangyang took Kang's bucket from Shaozhen and filled it halfway. Kang looked relieved when she didn't give it back to him but took claim of it as she wriggled back outside.

Despite the water they were carrying, they travelled faster on the way back, though the journey felt more treacherous. The water sloshing in their baskets constantly threw them off balance. Shaozhen felt short of breath as they picked their way down the steep rocks. His heart did flip-flops in his chest, but he was careful to stay as upright as he could, so as not to tip his precious cargo onto the dirt. Kang followed behind, muttering quiet prayers to the ancestors.

It was past lunch by the time they reached home and Shaozhen's stomach was grumbling. Yangyang went straight inside to store the water, muttering something about preparing cold noodles.

'Here's your water, Kang,' Shaozhen said as he handed his friend the bucket that Yangyang had left on the ground. Miraculously, most of the water was still in it. 'We'll make you a basket for next time. Then you can carry it more easily.'

Kang shook his head. 'I'm no good with labour work. Gung is right. I'm useless in the village.'

'But you're so smart and clever!' Shaozhen punched his friend in the arm to cheer him up.

Kang winced. 'I'd better go.' And with that, Kang headed home, holding the handle with both hands, the bucket banging against his knees and water sloshing up the sides.

Nine

A week later, and still no rain. Shaozhen was making his way to the mountain spring, struggling along the rocky path and pulling himself onto the narrow ledge. The daily trek up the mountains to collect water wasn't getting any easier and the beautiful spring that Yangyang had found was already running low. If they didn't find a new source of water soon, the village would go dry in a matter of weeks.

As he walked, his mind wandered. Master Chen had finally sent his exam results. He had passed, but just barely. There would be no scholarship for senior school next year. Nainai had simply shrugged it off and sent him to the fields, but Shaozhen was worried about telling his mother. He hated to disappoint her and without school, his fate of becoming a farmer seemed sealed.

Shaozhen paused as he reached the narrow cliff ledge. Yangyang had shown the villagers where to find water and they had all celebrated her as a hero. But now, with all the residents going back and forth between the village and the cave collecting water, the path had eroded and the journey was even tougher than before. Shaozhen still wasn't comfortable with this part of the trek, the sharp drop just a metre before him, but he'd learned to clamp down his fear. He took a deep breath and stepped gingerly onto the embankment.

He moved the wicker basket to his chest so he could press his back to the cliff face. He sucked in a deep breath and inched his way along. His footsteps sent small rocks and tiny pebbles down the steep embankment.

Suddenly, he heard a low rumbling and felt unsteady on his legs. Shaozhen froze, his stomach dropping as the sense of vertigo came over him. Silence. And then it came again. A prattling, rattling, getting louder and louder. Shaozhen realised that the shakiness wasn't coming from his legs but from the ground beneath his feet. The ledge was moving and Shaozhen felt like he was going to be thrown over the side.

A landslide. Shaozhen's whole body seized up with fear. His stomach turned as the ground kept swaying. He pushed back, toeing the edge of the slender shelf that he stood on, desperate to keep his back against the cliff. His breaths were shallow and ragged and his fingers grasped fruitlessly at the dirt and grass behind him, desperate for purchase. Pebbles and rocks were raining down all around him. Shaozhen squeezed his eyes shut and bit his lip so hard he tasted blood.

It felt like an eternity before the shaking stopped and things around him calmed. He waited, bow-legged and rickety, refusing to move. He felt like he might vomit, but he forced himself to scramble further along the path to safety.

Shaozhen collapsed on his hands and knees, panting for breath. The ground was solid here, the earth hard and sturdy, and he almost bent down to kiss it. It took a while before he could no longer hear the pounding in his ears.

He felt something wet running down his right leg and peered down. There was a crimson gash on his calf, about the length of his hand, where a sharp rock must have cut into it. Black dirt was caught in the wound. He winced as he tried to brush the grit off with his fingers, and he only managed to smear the blood over his leg.

Shaozhen tore off a part of his dirty T-shirt to fasten a bandage and try to stop the bleeding. Red seeped through the fabric but at least the blood was no longer trickling down his leg. He stood up slowly and made his way back to the ledge, hobbling as he tried not to put too much weight on his injured limb.

Landslides were a constant threat in the village but with the drought, it had been the furthest thing from everyone's minds. There had been no rains, no flooding, nor any other event that might trigger one. But Shaozhen knew that a landslide had the power to wipe out the village. Panic seized him. All thoughts of water were forgotten. He needed to get back to Hongsha – and fast.

Shaozhen picked his way carefully back down to the base of the mountain, his leg throbbing with every step. His mind raced, overcome by images of his grandmother, or even Yangyang, trapped under the rubble.

Are they at home or are they out in the fields? Is the house still standing? Has the landslide wiped out the entire village?

Half running, half stumbling, he made his way towards the village, dragging his right leg behind him. The bandage was a deep red colour now, completely soaked through.

Nainai! Nainai! He was willing his legs to go faster, wishing he had the height of Michael Jordan and the agility of John Starks. He was almost at the village entrance now, and he could hear the panicked voices of the farmers who were running back from the fields. He raced past Aunty Law, her straw hat askew on her head. 'Nainai! Nainai!' Shaozhen called out as he weaved among the villagers seeking out his grandmother.

The gates to the village headquarters were open and a crowd had gathered out the front. A few people were on their knees, wailing, as others tried to calm them down. Shaozhen ran towards them.

Finally, he spotted Nainai in the crowd. She was sobbing, her face buried in her hands as Yangyang tried to soothe her.

'Shaozhen!' His grandmother ran towards him, her tiny body moving like lightning. Shaozhen pushed through the crowd, ignoring the pain in his leg, until he finally collapsed into Nainai's arms, crying into her shoulders. She wrapped her arms around him like a thick rope and squeezed.

'Nainai.' Those were the only words he could manage through the tears. She kissed him as she cried and then she kissed him again.

'Shh. You're safe. We're all safe,' she murmured to him like she had when he was a toddler. She stroked his head and pressed her warm hand against the back of his neck. 'My precious grandson.' Shaozhen felt her tears dampening his skin. 'When we felt the landslide, I thought you were up there,' she sobbed.

He drew back to look at her face. 'And I thought it had hit the village.'

She shook her head. 'We're all fine.' And they clung to each other once again.

'Wah, you sure picked a ripe time to go up the mountain,' Yangyang declared from behind them. Shaozhen leapt up and threw his arms around her. He felt her body stiffen at first but then she returned the hug, happy to see him.

'Shaozhen!' Someone clapped him on the back, and he turned to see Chun. 'Yangyang said you were on the mountain. Did you see the landslide?'

'I felt it. Like the floor shaking. I thought the ground would break in two.' Nainai clamped her hand over her mouth like she was going to cry again. 'But I wasn't hurt at all,' he added quickly.

Nainai's gaze dropped to his right leg. 'What happened?' she wailed, inspecting the bright red bandage.

'It's okay, Nainai. I just cut myself on a rock. It looks worse than it is.' He tried not to wince as he bent over and undid the bandage. The T-shirt fabric seemed to cling to his leg as though it had tiny claws.

Nainai slapped his hand away and took over, her maternal nature kicking in. 'Yangyang, get a clean cloth and some water, quick,' she commanded. Yangyang rushed off and Nainai fussed over the wound.

Yangyang returned and Nainai had just about finished dressing his injury when the door to the headquarters opened.

'Hey, it's the Secretary,' said Chun.

The crowd pushed forwards, all clamouring at once. Secretary Xian's eyes went wide, like a hunted animal's, while he tried to make himself heard over the group.

'Please, comrades. Settle down.' But they didn't listen, trying to speak over each other.

'What is the Party going to do about the landslides?' someone asked.

'Is it still safe?' asked another. 'Will we have to move?'

Headmaster Song finally stepped between Xian and the group. 'Please, friends. Let's have some peace. Peace for the Secretary, please.'

'Thank you, Mr Song,' Xian stuttered, but he quickly composed himself. 'Comrades, I have spoken to Secretary Lam on the phone and our first and foremost priority is to ensure no residents have been hurt in the landslide. So, if any residents are unaccounted for, please speak up now so that we may send out a search party.'

Just then, there was a frantic voice from behind. The crowd turned. Aunty Wu was running towards them, her frizzy perm framing her face like the dried flowers they used for chrysanthemum tea. 'He's gone. He's gone! Xiaoping is missing!'

Shaozhen felt his stomach sink as Nainai started wailing beside him.

Ten

The crowd murmured anxiously as they took in the news. Aunty Wu was sobbing uncontrollably and Yangyang put an arm out to comfort her.

'Sit down, take a breath.' Headmaster Song led Aunty Wu to a concrete bench just inside the gate. 'What happened?' He offered the crying woman a handkerchief.

'We were on our way to the spring.' Aunty Wu blew her nose loudly before continuing. 'He was chasing a maque, sparrow, into someone's field and I lost sight of him in the short crop. I called his name, *Xiaoping! Xiaoping!* Nothing.

'And then I heard the rocks crashing down. I saw the dust. It was so close to our land. I started running, screaming his name, but he still didn't come. *Oh by the gods, where is my Xiaoping?*' she wailed. Nainai patted her on the back.

Shaozhen wiped his clammy hands on his shorts. He didn't want to imagine where Xiaoping might be.

'Aunty Wu, please don't despair,' Xian said quietly. 'We'll send teams out to look for him straightaway.'

Song organised them into search parties and Xian insisted on commanding one. Shaozhen was teamed with Kang, Yangyang and Tingming, and the four of them traversed the rows of crops in the Wu family's plot, using sticks to push the plants aside, in case the toddler was hiding between them.

The air felt dark and foreboding as they traipsed through the fields, calling out his name.

'Xiaoping!'

'XIAOPING!'

Only the dry breeze answered, hot and harsh like it was mocking them.

The afternoon dragged on and there was no sign of Xiaoping. A few of the search parties went back to the village headquarters but Shaozhen and his friends refused to go. They went from field to field, up and down the rows of wilting corn – everything looked the same and Shaozhen lost track of whose land was whose. The sun was hot and scorching, beating down on them. Shaozhen felt his heart squeezing as he called out the boy's name, over and over, until his throat was raw.

Finally, he sank to his knees. 'This is hopeless,' he called out to Kang. He tried to block out the flashes of Xiaoping, buried in rubble from the landslide, that kept leaping into his mind.

'Don't give up now. Come on, he needs you.' Kang had been quiet for most of the search, but now there was a look of intense concentration on his face.

Kang squatted down beside Shaozhen and closed his eyes. 'I'm little Xiaoping.' He used the back of his hand to push up his glasses. 'I've come up from the fields. I'm lost by myself. And I hear rumbling. A landslide. Where would I go?' he wondered aloud.

Shaozhen thought about this for a moment. 'If *I* was three, I would want my parents. But his parents are in the city.'

'What about somewhere that reminded him of his parents?' Kang suggested. 'Somewhere he might feel safe. What did his parents do?'

'His father was a farmer, just like the rest of us,' Shaozhen said. 'He used to collect mushrooms in the forest. But Xiaoping's probably too young to remember his father taking him camping in the…'

In an instant he was up and running, his feet feeling light as he charged on with a newfound energy. 'Of course, why didn't I think of it earlier? Yangyang! Tingming!' he called, and they came running over. 'Do you think he might have gone on to the mountains? Aunty Wu said they were on their way there. They might have been close. Plus his father used to take him there all the time.'

'It makes sense,' Yangyang said. 'It's cooler there too. We should look.'

Tingming nodded. 'It's a good idea. Everyone's been so focused on the fields, I bet no one's even thought to go up the mountains.' Shaozhen hid his annoyance as the older boy took the lead.

The four of them rushed past more fields. They

eventually reached the steps; it wasn't hard to picture a little boy trying to climb up them on his own. They raced upwards, taking the stairs two at a time. Shaozhen felt his heart pumping faster and faster, his eyes anxiously scanning the skies for falling rocks and debris.

'There, look.' Yangyang pointed at the path that led to the hut. 'Do you think he went up there?'

'We should split up, cover more ground,' Tingming said. 'Yangyang, Kang, you two go that way and Shaozhen and I'll head to the spring. Let's meet back at the village.'

The spring. Shaozhen felt his whole body tense remembering the earth shuddering beneath his feet. 'Ah, maybe I should go with Kang? I wanted to have a look at the house before.'

Tingming shrugged. 'If you're scared, you don't have to go. I can go myself.' And he disappeared down the path alone.

'I'm not scared,' Shaozhen said a bit too loudly, though he was quite relieved he wouldn't have to go back towards the spring. He just hated that Tingming thought he was a coward.

But there were more important things to think about. The trio headed up the rocky track, Shaozhen leading the way through the dense undergrowth at the base of the trees. He trailed his hand across the stiff dry bark of a narrow trunk. The tree seemed sickly, like one gentle tap would snap it in two.

He mustered a deep breath from the pit of his stomach and shouted, 'Xiaoping!'

His voice echoed thinly before vanishing into the canopy. He rubbed his upper arms but it did nothing to ebb the chill going through his heart.

The ground levelled off and Shaozhen heard a goat bleating. He could see a trail leading to a small vegetable garden that looked well-cared-for. Beyond the garden, there was the open door that led to a home. And it was clear to him now that the house wasn't abandoned.

And sitting on the doorstep was Xiaoping, dirt smeared on his chubby cheeks and the remnants of a crumbled cracker in his pudgy fist.

'Xiaoping!' Shaozhen ran towards the boy.

'Dage! Big brother!' Xiaoping's eyes lit up and he smiled wide, wet clumps of biscuit stuck to his teeth. Shaozhen wrapped the boy up in a giant panda-sized hug.

'Thank goodness we found you! How did you get all the way up here?' he murmured.

'The mountain man woke up today!' Xiaoping cried. 'He was cranky! So I hid but then Shen Yeye found me.' His breath smelled of goat's milk and biscuit.

'Man, I really hate these mountains,' Kang complained as he came up the trail past the garden.

'Who would be living all the way up here by themselves?' Yangyang wondered aloud. But their complaints were silenced when they saw who Shaozhen held in his arms.

'Kang ge, elder brother! Yang jie, elder sister!' Xiaoping smiled and waved but he stayed in Shaozhen's arms.

'Thank goodness he's okay.' Yangyang reached out to stroke the toddler on the head, cooing affectionately. 'You had your grandmother so worried, you know?'

'Pingping, who's there?' A sinister voice came from inside the house.

Shaozhen took a few steps back, clutching the boy to his chest. An old man with a cane emerged from the house and came onto the front stoop.

'Yeye!' Xiaoping reached for the man but Shaozhen kept him in his embrace.

'Oh, the villagers found you now, did they? About time.' He eyed the teens for a moment, his expression unreadable. 'Off you go then,' he said with a wave of his cane.

'Wait, laoba, old father,' Shaozhen called. The man turned, his eyes narrowing and his jaw jutting out. He was slight and his demeanour so fierce and ferocious that Shaozhen stammered, 'I mean, I wanted to thank you for looking after Xiaoping.'

The old man remained silent.

Kang stepped forwards, putting on his best Number One Pupil's voice. 'What Shaozhen means, honourable sir, is that Hongsha village would like to thank you for looking after our young friend. And I'm sure once we inform Secretary Xian, he will want to come and thank you too.'

At the mention of the Secretary, the man's eyes bugged out. 'You keep those Secretaries away from me,' he spat. 'We've kept to ourselves for twenty years and it had better stay that way. Or I'll send the rocks down to flatten your lot myself.' He stomped one foot on the ground and thrashed his cane. It let out a thunderous crack that boomed across the mountains and Yangyang yelped. Shaozhen winced, imagining the sound setting off another landslide, but nothing happened.

'Get out of here now, and don't let me see any of you ever again!'

Shaozhen hurried away, pressing Xiaoping to his shoulder.

'Bye bye, Shen Yeye, grandfather! I hope you can come back to Hongsha soon.' Xiaoping waved what was left of his soggy biscuit. He didn't seem to mind the old man's sudden change in attitude.

Shaozhen just shook his head. 'Come on, let's get you back to Aunty Wu.'

⬤⬤⬤

The sun had set by the time they reached the village. The villagers all gasped and sighed with relief when they saw the teens coming through the entrance, the toddler almost asleep and drooling on Shaozhen's shoulder.

'Xiaoping!' Aunty Wu had fat tears running down her puffy red cheeks as she took the boy from Shaozhen's arms and gave him a big wet kiss. 'Oh, you were such a naughty boy today. Wait until your mother finds out you ran away from me, huh?' She bounced the boy against her hip and then turned to Shaozhen. 'Precious boy. Dear boy. Thank you for bringing my grandson back. You are an absolute hero.' She reached up and pinched Shaozhen on the cheek, like he was seven. He winced but didn't really mind, he was so relieved and happy to have found Xiaoping.

'That's okay, Aunty Wu,' Shaozhen said. 'We're just glad he's okay.'

'Yangyang, thank you so much.'

Yangyang smiled modestly, her face dimpling.

'Kang, I know your grandfather will be really proud,' Aunty Wu added.

Kang lowered his gaze to the ground, embarrassed. Shaozhen knew his friend wasn't used to praise.

'Popo, I'm tired.' Xiaoping rubbed his eyes, smearing dirt across his face.

'You've had a long day, darling. Time for bed.' Aunty Wu bid them goodnight before setting off, the toddler drifting off to sleep on her shoulder.

The other villagers made their way back to their houses. Shaozhen felt the exhaustion deep in every one of his muscles and there was a dull ache through his leg, but he wasn't ready to go back just yet. He was still wondering about the old man, Shen, living by himself in the mountains. Had he really been there for twenty years? He had said 'we'. Did someone else live up there with him? His mind swam with unanswered questions.

Kang pointed towards the road. 'Hey, look. Tingming is back.'

Shaozhen turned. He had completely forgotten about Tingming. He cocked an eyebrow as the older boy hurried towards them. His face was flushed and the usual swagger in his step was gone.

'What's the matter, Tingming?' Yangyang's voice was full of concern. 'Don't worry, we found Xiaoping.'

The older boy shook his head. 'It's not that. We have big problems.'

Kang's eyes went wide. 'What do you mean?'

The older boy rubbed the back of his neck. 'I tried to go up the path to the spring, but it was blocked by boulders, and there's no way to get to the other side.'

'But I was only there this morning, out on the ledge.' Shaozhen shuddered as he remembered standing on that narrow ridge, the earth shaking beneath him.

Tingming shook his head. 'It was further along, right before the cave, just at the mouth of it, actually. It's completely cut off. You're very lucky, Shaozhen.'

There was silence as they all took in the news. Kang looked at Shaozhen like he was about to cry. Yangyang, always strong and fearless, looked very, very afraid. Shaozhen felt entirely numb; the only sensation left was the dull throbbing in his injured leg.

Without another word, they all knew that Hongsha's biggest fear had come true.

Eleven

Tingming's discovery sent shockwaves through the residents of Hongsha. Without the spring, there was no source of clean water. This was much worse than the water shortages had ever been before.

When he returned home, Shaozhen pried off the cover to the storage container and peered inside. Tiny particles of dirt swirled in the half-filled bucket. He thought back to the old woman at the stream. Once it ran dry, there wouldn't even be river muck to drink!

Shaozhen lay on his unmade bed, staring up at the bare walls, lobbing the basketball into the air until it almost hit the ceiling and then catching it. The pigs squealed outside under his window but he had the curtains drawn. His heart thumped in his chest, his mind consumed with worry. He had tossed and turned all night, his mind playing out the landslide, the search for Xiaoping and finally the realisation that the spring was cut off. He missed Ma; her soothing voice had an amazing calming effect that could even take the edge off Nainai's angriest tirades. He felt a tugging between his eyes and he blinked rapidly, refusing to cry. Instead he switched on the gas lamp in his room then reached under his bed and tore a sheet of notebook paper from an old schoolbook and began to write.

Dear Ma and Ba,

How are you? I haven't received a letter from you in a month. I have been helping Nainai and Yangyang in the fields but there is still no water. Sometimes the pigs have to go thirsty.

There is a new Village Secretary in Hongsha. His name is Xian and he comes from Chengdu. He just graduated from university.

I passed my exams. Master Chen was very impressed. If I can go to senior school and then university, maybe we can all live in the city together? Wouldn't that be great.

I miss you both. I've tried to call you at the factory from Aunty Law's but no one ever picks up the phone. I hope you can call or write or come home soon.
Your loving son,
Shaozhen

Shaozhen paused, gnawing on the tip of his pencil as he considered the half-told truth about his grades. He had passed, so it wasn't a complete lie – although it was definitely a stretch to say Master Chen had been impressed.

He was about to rub out the sentence when the loudspeakers over at the village headquarters suddenly crackled to life. Shaozhen put down his pencil as Secretary Xian's timid voice washed over the residences.

'Comrades, friends. The Party requests that all residents assemble outside the village headquarters in thirty minutes to discuss official matters. Attendance is mandatory. That is all.'

Shaozhen, Yangyang and Nainai joined the masses gathering outside the headquarters. Everyone was talking about the spring being cut off. As the group grew larger, the discussions became more agitated.

'The Party should do something!' Lao Zhu declared, peppering his words with spittle. 'But they don't care about us poor villagers. They're so busy furnishing their government-issued apartments in Beijing that they don't even have time to fix the broken window at the school!'

'You know what I heard?' another man remarked. 'They're building some crazy machine that pumps the water to the North.'

'They moved the clouds away from Beijing for the Olympics. So they could take photos!' someone else said.

Secretary Xian and Headmaster Song emerged from the village headquarters and the group began clamouring.

'Headmaster Song, you have to save us. You need to get us water!' Aunty Law shouted.

Before Song could answer, the Secretary raised his hands, demanding silence. 'My fellow comrades,' he began. 'As you know, Headmaster Song and myself have brought up the issue of the water with Secretary Lam. With the most recent landslide, our access to alternative sources has been—'

'Enough, boy. Where's the water?' someone shouted.

'Yeah, why isn't Lam here? Doesn't he care about his residents enough to show his face?' There were shouts of agreement. Secretary Xian turned bright red.

'Friends, please!' Headmaster Song stepped up and the crowd fell silent straightaway, eager to hear him speak.

'Secretary Xian has done an incredible job speaking to the Party on our behalf. I could tell Secretary Lam was genuinely moved by Xian's heartfelt plea. He did a fantastic job. The Town Magistrate even congratulated him for his commitment and devoted service.' Song's words calmed the crowd and Xian toed the ground with the tip of his worn leather shoe.

'But what did Lam have to say for himself? And what about our water?' The worried voice was Aunty Wu's, who held a squirming little Xiaoping in her arms.

Xian lifted his chin and faced the group. 'Secretary Lam sends his support and congratulates the Hongsha residents on their resilience in the face of hardship. He says your Henan spirit is exemplary.' He paused before continuing. 'As for the water, the Secretary has already arranged for provisions. Hongsha residents are welcome to fetch water daily from the trucks that will be driven to Xifeng.'

'*Xifeng?* We have to go all the way to Xifeng for water? Unbelievable!' Mongsok spat.

'How am I supposed to get there with my bad knees?' a man with a cane chimed in. 'I'm not a young man anymore.'

The group was getting rowdier, hurling questions and complaints at Xian, but they quietened when a new voice called out, 'Villagers, please.' It was Wang Daifu, the village doctor. He was an old man but he carried himself tall and straight, not hunched over like so many of the farmers who spent their lives bent double in the fields. He had a quiet manner about him and never used ten words when two would do. He had been involved in every birth, every death and every matter of illness across Hongsha.

When Wang Daifu spoke, the villagers listened.

'Villagers, I understand your disappointment. I too was hoping that we would be delivered a Party miracle to fill our jugs and save our crops. But let's be reasonable. There has been no rain here for more than two months. Do you think the officials in Xifeng have their own rain clouds?

'The drought has affected not just our village but the entire province and beyond, as far even as Mongolia. All the businesses that use water have closed, including many restaurants. Headmaster Song, didn't we see that the town bathhouse was boarded shut?'

Song nodded. 'And all the cars were dirty, even the high officials'.'

'That's right,' Wang Daifu said. 'And in the fancy new city apartments there's no water. Families are carrying bottles many li just so they can drink. Everyone is making a sacrifice, that is the community way. So surely we as a village can see fit to travel a few hours to fetch water for our dying crops and thirsty cattle? To do what we can to help ourselves?'

The crowd was silent as they listened to Wang Daifu. Shaozhen started to feel a little guilty for thinking it would be too far to travel. The Party was delivering all the water they needed for free – and all they had to do was go and get it.

The doctor and the headmaster exchanged a look, the same grim smiles on their faces. 'Good, it is settled,' Song declared. 'Tomorrow morning, we head to Xifeng. We will carry water on our backs and work hard on the farmland, just like our ancestors before us. And together, we will deliver a bountiful harvest and put together a feast fit for the great emperors.'

The villagers murmured in agreement, though Shaozhen could tell that more than a few were swallowing their dissent. But what other choice did they have?

⚫⚫⚫

The next morning, the entire village was up before dawn. They scurried from their homes like eager ants running towards a spoonful of sugar water left out in the sun. The younger villagers had strong bamboo poles slung on their backs, while the elderly carried buckets in their hands. Tingming and Wulei had both fashioned a double-tier system on their poles, so that they could each carry four ten-gallon drums. One of the older women had a small infant strapped to her front in a pouch, while she carried her water pole over her shoulders. Little Xiaoping was skipping along under the hawk-eye watch of Aunty Wu.

The trio from the Lu household set off. Yangyang led the way, her wicker basket bouncing against her back and two large buckets dangling from her pole. Not to be outdone, Shaozhen carried the same load. He hardly felt the weight anymore. The weeks he had spent out in the fields and hauling water from the mountains had made him considerably stronger. Nainai followed behind.

As they headed up the road, Shaozhen saw Kang, struggling with two oversized buckets on a pole slung across his back. He was too short, and the bottom of the buckets were scraping along the ground. Once they were filled with water, it would be impossible for him to carry them back on his own.

'Hey, Kang, let's trade,' Shaozhen suggested, handing over his pole fitted with slightly smaller buckets.

Kang swapped with a sigh of relief. 'Gung wants to sell water at the shop. If I don't bring extra back, he says he'll burn my books.'

Shaozhen's heart ached for his friend. Kang's gung seemed almost heartless at times, much stricter than Nainai ever was.

The villagers forged a line down the road towards Xifeng, a giant procession of limbs and buckets, young and old. Fortunately, the road into the town had just a few gentle inclines, nothing like the treacherous climb up the mountain. While a few of the villagers powered ahead, clearly wanting to get to Xifeng before the rest, most families set off at a leisurely pace, so the hundred or so villagers were moving as a group, like a slow, winding snake. Shaozhen licked his dry cracked lips, enjoying the quiet camaraderie of their procession.

'Come on, you old siyuyan, dead fish eyes, who knows a joke?' Aunty Law called out.

'I know one but I wouldn't say it in front of the children,' Mongsok snorted.

'How about this one?' Headmaster Song asked, his eyebrows dancing with delight. 'There are twenty-six letters in the English alphabet. If you take away two of them, E and T, how many letters would there be left?'

'Twenty-four, of course,' said Aunty Wu.

'Ah you're wrong. Because ET would leave with UFO!' The headmaster erupted into a fit of laughter, slapping his thigh with delight. The rest of the group remained stony-faced and wondering, although Shaozhen saw Kang crack a smile.

Aunty Law wasn't deterred. 'All right, how about a song then? Chinese-opera style.' She broke into a lilting melody, the notes alternating from high to low, short and drawn out.

'Wah, Aunty Law, any more singing and the birds will be dropping dead from the trees,' cried Mongsok.

Aunty Law laughed but the comment didn't faze her. And at some point, the headmaster joined her in song, and then a few of the other villagers followed suit. Lovely baritones and altos mixed in with Aunty Law's strained soprano. Shaozhen and Yangyang didn't know the song but Nainai hummed along.

It would have been around eight when they arrived at the boundary of the township. Shaozhen had expected a few people to be out at this time of day. With the local middle school, a hospital and a small canning factory, Xifeng was always a hub of activity.

But he and the rest of the villagers were in for a shock.

Twelve

Masses of people had gathered along the road. The shops on the main street were yet to open, but there were hundreds of men, women and children all like them, carrying long poles and buckets, some rolling drums. Shaozhen had seen large crowds in the town before, but never like this. There were even a few vehicles about, mostly sanlun, three-wheeled motorcycles, the preferred farmer's transport that consisted of a flatbed trailer bolted onto the back of a moped frame. Every trailer was overloaded with gallon drums and plastic buckets. The drivers stood around looking bored as if they had been waiting for a long time.

At the end of the road was the junior middle school that Shaozhen and Kang went to. It was hard to imagine he had been taking his final exams only a few weeks ago.

The water truck was nowhere to be seen. A couple of officials were trying to create order, shouting and waving short batons at the crowd as they pushed forwards.

'Please form a queue. There won't be room for the truck if you don't clear the way.'

The villagers stood there, stunned, and unsure of how to enter the fray. Shaozhen was suddenly shy, even though a part of him considered Xifeng to be his home.

'You new arrivals – go to the back of the queue,' an official barked, ushering them off the road. 'The truck will arrive soon. Remember, only two buckets per household.'

The official spotted Tingming and Wulei, each with their four hanging buckets. 'You boys live together?' He didn't give them a chance to reply. 'You'll only be able to take home two,' he shouted, holding up two fingers.

'What? Only two buckets?' Yangyang fingered the straps of the woven basket on her back, her eyes darting from her own buckets to Nainai and Shaozhen's.

Tingming slammed his pole to the ground and stormed over to the official. 'Are you kidding me? We came all the way from Hongsha, near the base of the mountain, and you say *two buckets*?'

The official nodded. 'That's right. The order is from Secretary Lam himself. Two buckets per household. If you want more, you'll have to come back for the next truck.'

'Come back?' Tingming balled his fists by his side.

Shaozhen shifted his buckets nervously. He didn't want Tingming to cause trouble for them. 'Come on, Tingming,' he said quietly. 'We should join the queue before it gets any longer.'

But the older boy wouldn't budge. 'Didn't you hear him? It takes at least ninety minutes each way. There won't be time to come back for the next truck!' Tingming shook his head in frustration, but then, to Shaozhen's relief, he retrieved his buckets from the ground.

The official sneered and gestured to the buckets Shaozhen was carrying for Kang. 'And, boy, those are much too big. You'll only be able to fill up one.'

Tingming opened his mouth to protest but Shaozhen steered him away.

Kang moaned. 'I'm going to be in so much trouble.'

Two buckets. Shaozhen shook his head, looking from his buckets to Yangyang's and Nainai's. Two buckets per household wasn't much at all. They might have water to drink and cook with, but then there were the pigs to feed and the corn was still dying in the fields.

They heard the slow rumbling of an approaching engine. The officials did their best to shift the hordes to the edges of the road, banging their sticks against their palms and shouting, 'Move to the side. Make way.'

Shaozhen had imagined a truck with sixteen wheels, barrels stacked three metres tall, chock-full of water.

But this was just an ordinary fire truck that wasn't much bigger than the vehicles that came around to the villages come harvest time. It was old and worn, its tyres sagging into the ground. The freshly painted words 'Xifeng Township Fire Rescue Authority' looked out of place against the faded reddish pink on the side. The engine stuttered as the driver backed into the lane, his shiny bald head hanging out of the window. He paused to hack a lurgy and spit on the ground.

'Make way, people. Form two lines,' one of the officials shouted, shooing stragglers off the road. Another was trying to guide the truck into place but he wasn't really looking, just flapping his gloved hand. The truck veered to the left and the right, stopped and then started, until, finally, the driver switched off the engine and pulled the parking brake into place.

People began unfastening their buckets from their poles, hugging them close to their bodies like newborn children. The driver and a second man got out of the truck and moved to the back of the vehicle. The driver was holding a length of plastic tubing and he jammed one end into a spout fastened to the base of the truck. The other man had a long metal wrench that he positioned over the nut on the top of the spout, before giving it a mighty tug.

And with that, a clear trickle of water began to run out of the tube and onto the ground.

'Wah, don't waste it!' The man at the head of the queue shoved his bucket under the water to catch the flow. The front of the mob surged forwards, buckets at the ready, jostling each other to get as close to the stream as possible until one of the officials ordered them back into the queue. The men then opened up another spout on the other side of the truck. 'I'm going to go over there,' Yangyang declared. But it didn't take long for the mob to crowd in and she found herself caught in the back.

'Remember, two buckets per household. That's all.' The officials were trying to maintain some semblance of authority, waving their batons through the air. But the people began policing each other as the buckets filled up.

'Dong, I saw your grandson carrying off two buckets already,' a woman scolded the hunchbacked man behind her in the queue. 'You've had your share.'

'I've walked four hours to get here. Don't let it be for nothing. Just one bucket and I won't come tomorrow.'

'Two buckets per household, that's it. Move along,' said the driver.

Shaozhen watched the progression, his palms getting sweaty as he gripped the handles of the buckets and waited his turn. The stream seemed to be easing off, like the truck was emptying. *Will there be enough?* He felt the crowd tightening around him in reply.

Finally, they reached the front. The driver didn't even look at them, just snatched the proffered buckets from Nainai's hands and placed them under the stream. The basket itched on Shaozhen's back and he wondered about offering it to be filled, but the hard stare from the official beside him made up his mind.

Suddenly a strong hand gripped his arm. Nainai was doubled over beside him, her free hand at her waist, pain evident on her face.

'Nainai, what's wrong?' He draped her arm over his shoulders to support her weight. 'You look pale. Why don't you go sit down?' He started leading her away from the truck.

She leant into him but she shook her head. 'No, I'm okay. We need the water.' Her voice was weak and she was short of breath and she dropped the pole she was carrying.

'Next bucket,' the driver called out and the people were pushing against them, trying to reach the water. Shaozhen gripped his grandmother around her tiny waist and they stumbled away from the group. Nainai's face was ghostly white, her eyes half-closed.

'Nainai?' Shaozhen fought the urge to shake her like a doll.

Just then Yangyang was at their side. 'Come on, Nainai. We'll go sit down. Shaozhen can get the water.'

Shaozhen recognised the fear in Yangyang's eyes but he went back to retrieve their buckets. The two white pails had once held cooking oil and the Lu family had used them for hauling water since last summer. Shaozhen spotted them straightaway: they were being hoisted onto the shoulder of a muscly man in a tattered flannel shirt.

Shaozhen tapped the man on the shoulder. 'Excuse me. Those are mine.'

The man turned and peered down at him, the edges of his mouth turning up to reveal black rings around his teeth. The man didn't say a word, just shifted the weight of the buckets, his gaze fixed on Shaozhen.

'Hey! Give those back.' Shaozhen leant over and smacked the man's hands, trying to slap the buckets away. He heard the crack of his palms against rock-like knuckles. It was like hitting steel rods.

'Watch your hands there, boy.' The man leered, revealing grey, sodden gums above the grim teeth.

'Hey, you're stealing my buckets. I left them there so I could help my grandmother.'

'These are my buckets, dirty village boy. I carried them here from my home and I'm going to carry them back.'

'You're lying!' Shaozhen was shouting now, his hands clenched into fists, the left one throbbing. He tried to pull himself taller and meet the man's gaze. He couldn't keep his knees from shaking.

'Shaozhen, is everything all right?' Headmaster Song appeared from the crowd. He caught Shaozhen's eye before turning to address the man. His voice was calm and steady. 'Sir, I believe there must be some mistake. This young lad is from my village and I saw him carry these buckets here this morning. Perhaps your buckets look very similar, but I can assure you—'

The man laughed. 'Get a load of this tubao, country bumpkin, trying to tell me I've made a mistake.' He slung the pole over one shoulder, letting the weights of the buckets swing freely. 'These are my buckets, little man, and this is my water, and I suggest you mind your own business if you know what's good for you.'

Song stammered in protest but stepped back into the crowd.

The man turned to leave but there was a thunderous crack. Tingming had appeared, bamboo pole in hand, his eyes wide and his mouth pulled back into a snarl. He raised the pole, ready to strike the earth with it once again. 'I hope you're not thinking of going anywhere with those.'

The man stood his ground, but Shaozhen saw the shift in his expression.

'I'm warning you.' Tingming raised one end of his pole so that it was level with the man's wide forehead. One swift thrust and he could drive it into him like a branding iron. 'Now, why don't you set those buckets down and move along.'

'You're nothing but tubaozi,' said the man.

'Don't call him tubao.' Shaozhen tried to keep his voice strong. He took a step forwards, sidling over to Tingming's side, and raised his fists in an attempt to look menacing.

The man's eyes darted from left to right as a small group began to form around them. Two village boys facing off against a grown man who was almost twice the size of one of them made for quite a spectacle.

With a grunt, the man threw the buckets down, water sloshing everywhere as he huffed away. Shaozhen let out a gasp of relief and he rushed over to the buckets. His hands were shaking as he attempted to hoist the rod over his shoulders. Buckets secure, he turned back awkwardly to his saviour.

'Thanks, Tingming,' he mumbled.

The older boy shrugged. 'You would have done the same. In times of hardship, we watch our brothers' backs.' He offered his hand, which Shaozhen shook after a moment's hesitation.

Tingming cracked a smile. 'See you on the court.'

Shaozhen chuckled but then remembered Nainai and quickly excused himself. He moved as swiftly as he could, taking extra care not to spill the water he had almost lost.

His grandmother was sitting up on a small step. Yangyang was fanning her with a scrap of an old flyer.

'Seriously, Yangyang, I am fine.' Nainai tried to push the girl's hand away.

'You almost fainted! You need air. And water. Where's – oh look, there he is, thank goodness.' Yangyang waved Shaozhen closer. 'You got the water.'

'Yeah.' Shaozhen was about to recount his and Tingming's heroics, but thought better of it. He watched Yangyang plunge a hand into the bucket and bring water up to Nainai's lips.

'Laobo, drink,' she commanded.

Nainai protested at first, but eventually slurped the water. When she was done, Yangyang sucked the droplets from between her fingers.

'Nainai, are you okay?' Shaozhen asked. Despite their weight, he kept a firm hold on the buckets, not wanting to let them out of his sight again.

His grandmother gazed up into his eyes. The colour had returned to her cheeks and she was smiling a little, although she still seemed frail. 'I'm okay, just a silly bout of dizziness. Here, let me help you.'

Shaozhen shook his head violently and shrugged his shoulders to keep the pole balanced. 'Yangyang, you and Nainai take your time going back to the village. I'm going to rush home. Maybe if I come back for the next truck, they'll let me have two more buckets.'

Yangyang nodded and Shaozhen took off. His feet felt light despite the load he carried. He whistled tunelessly as he walked, trying to match the chirruping of the birds. He was feeling cheerful and triumphant. Two buckets of water wasn't much, but after almost coming away with none, it somehow felt like a fortune.

Thirteen

Shaozhen and Yangyang took it in turns to rise with the birds and hike to Xifeng to wait for the water truck. Nainai always tried to come along, but they insisted she stayed home to rest. Despite their best efforts, every afternoon, one of them would come home with just two buckets. They did what they could to make the water last, using half a bucket for drinking and cooking.

The electric jug went unfilled – there was no more tea to be made. Cooking was a challenge; there wasn't enough water for rice or boiling noodles. Instead, Yangyang made do with the scrawny vegetables from the garden. But the fibre from the withered stalks was rough on their digestive system without much water to wash it down. Shaozhen sometimes felt like he was passing a basketball through his bowels.

He knew the other villagers blamed Secretary Xian. 'That good-for-nothing child is just a pawn of Lam. He's done nothing to help our situation,' they complained.

'We'd rather have Luqiao – he was a crook but at least he had some backbone.'

Headmaster Song did his best to support the new Secretary. 'The drought has affected the entire province. What can one man do when all the villages are clamouring for the same thing?' But the villagers weren't listening.

Every day, Secretary Xian left the house on a rickety bicycle and cycled to Xifeng to meet with Secretary Lam. The villagers pointed and sneered at him, hurling insults and shaking their fists as he rode past. Xian's face stayed like stone but Shaozhen felt sorry for the Secretary. One time, he saw Xian wiping his face with the back of his arm; Shaozhen was pretty certain it wasn't sweat that he was mopping up.

As the weeks wore on, the villagers became more agitated. The heat from the sun was torture, as if they were all trapped in a giant oven. The two buckets of water per day no longer felt like a fortune. Even the most steadfast and determined farmers had stopped going to the fields every day. There was no point, everything was dying. Some of the villagers went back to mountains, hoping they'd find a new path to the spring or an alternative source of water. But there was nothing.

Without water, there would be no harvest. Without income from the farm that year, the Lu family would be completely reliant on his parents' wages. Shaozhen knew that senior school fees were expensive; the thought of it knotted his gut and filled him with worry. Despite her promise, Ma hadn't written since she had left for

Guangzhou. There had been one hurried phone call she'd made from the factory floor. Shaozhen's family didn't have their own home phone so she had called Aunty Law's house instead. Shaozhen had rushed to take the call, eager to hear his ma's voice after all this time. But the line was bad and the background so noisy that it had been impossible to exchange more than a quick hello. His father was too busy for even a greeting. Shaozhen had choked back tears when he finally hung up.

Harvest time was now four weeks away, but instead of the usual buzz of excitement, the residents of Hongsha were fraught with worry. The atmosphere in the queue to the water truck was changing. Instead of the singing camaraderie from that first morning, the villagers were all weary with the constant back and forth. The line was getting longer as more and more communities had to fetch their water from Xifeng. Shaozhen noticed a number of villagers had started having tense encounters with the townsfolk. The Xifeng residents saved spots for each other in the queue every morning, pushing the outsiders to the back, no matter how early they arrived. Shaozhen had seen the man who almost stole his buckets a couple of times. The man had leered at him, like a cat contemplating its next meal. Shaozhen kept his distance. He wasn't eager for a repeat of the previous standoff without the help of Tingming.

While the villagers were blaming the Village Secretary, Shaozhen still had faith in Xian and his plans for the village. He recalled their conversation in Xian's home. *I want to help the residents of Hongsha achieve a better future for themselves.*

Shaozhen just hoped Xian would make it happen sooner rather than later.

❋❋❋

Shaozhen was coming home from Xifeng, his allotted two buckets in tow. Yangyang had come with him that morning to sell the last of the pigs. There was hardly any water left for thirsty people, let alone thirsty pigs. The truck had been late and everyone had been extra grouchy queuing in the hot sun. On the way home, Secretary Xian overtook them on the road, pedalling towards Hongsha on his pushbike.

'Xian,' Shaozhen called out. But the young man didn't stop so Shaozhen called louder. 'Xian. Secretary Xian.'

But still the Secretary didn't turn. Shaozhen started running, waving his free arm, the buckets at the end of his pole rocking from side to side. His toe caught on a sharp rock and he stumbled.

'Shaozhen!' Yangyang cried out, but it was too late.

Precious water was pooling on the ground. The Secretary had pedalled away, oblivious. Shaozhen felt his shoulders sag and his heart empty.

'Shaozhen.' Yangyang's voice was tiny. 'How could you?'

He had no answer.

The pair managed to save some of the buckets' contents but Yangyang wouldn't say a word to him for the rest of the walk home. Shaozhen felt the extra weight of his shame on his shoulders. How was he going to explain this to Nainai?

But when they got home, there was a bigger problem than the lack of water.

◉◉◉

When the pair arrived at the front door they heard a soft moan from inside the house.

Shaozhen threw open the door to his bedroom. Nainai was sprawled on the ground, limbs akimbo.

'Nainai, what happened?' he cried in dismay as they both rushed to her side.

Nainai smiled, the relief unmistakable on her face. 'Oh dear child, it's nothing. I just fell. What a clumsy old lady I am.' They grabbed her arms and she made an effort to push herself up but winced in pain.

'Don't move. Stay here. I'll go get the doctor!' Shaozhen raced outside, his bare feet padding along the dirt.

'Wang Daifu!' he shouted. He rapped on the doctor's door and a light winked on. 'Wang Daifu, please, come quickly.'

The startled doctor pulled open the door.

'Wang Daifu, please. It's my nainai. She fell.'

Wang Daifu's eyes widened and he sprang into action. He grabbed a small bag beside the door and followed Shaozhen back to his house.

When they arrived, Yangyang was kneeling in Shaozhen's bedroom, pressing a wet washcloth to

Nainai's forehead. Nainai winced. There was no question that she was in a lot of pain. She gave the old doctor a brave smile.

'Oh, Wang Daifu. I'm sorry to be such a nuisance to you today.'

'Don't be silly, Lu-sum, ma'am,' the doctor said affectionately as he stooped to examine her. He laid a hand against her pelvis and she let out a wail of pain. He frowned.

'Hmm, I fear you may have broken your hip,' he said with concern. Yangyang cried out in alarm and Nainai moaned again. The doctor turned to Shaozhen. 'Your nainai needs to go to the hospital in Xifeng. We're going to need a car.'

Shaozhen's mind raced. 'Secretary Xian. He has a car. A truck, actually. I saw it parked outside his house.'

The doctor nodded. 'Better go up there quickly and ask.'

Shaozhen felt his heart ricocheting inside his chest as he ran as fast as he could towards the Secretary's house. He paused briefly when he remembered the Secretary pedalling away on his bike earlier that day. Was Xian ignoring him? Why had he never seen him drive if he had a vehicle? Was this a waste of time? He tried to push the thoughts away; his nainai needed him.

Shaozhen stomped through the courtyard, the fine gravel crunching beneath his feet, and up the steps to the mirrored doors. He was relieved to see the truck he had seen the first night he had visited was parked out front.

He banged loud and fast, calling out, 'Xian! Secretary Xian!'

A pale face poked out of the doorway and blinked at Shaozhen. Xian's face was gaunt and white, with puffy bags under his eyes like he hadn't been sleeping.

'Shaozhen.' The Secretary sounded as haggard as he looked. Shaozhen felt a wave of pity wash over him. 'What are you doing here?'

'Xian. Secretary, I mean,' Shaozhen stammered. He had barely spoken to the Secretary since the time they'd had tea. He was suddenly overcome with a need for formality. 'It's my nainai. She's hurt very badly and Wang Daifu has asked if we may borrow your truck to transport her to the hospital in town. She's in a lot of pain.'

Shaozhen was hoping Xian would leap into action. But instead, he just nodded, then tilted his chin like an imperial scholar.

'I see. And the transporting of your nainai – would you consider this to be a Party matter?'

Shaozhen was stunned. 'She's my grandmother. I – I don't know. Luqiao used to lend his car to some of the villagers, I thought...'

Xian stood up straighter at the mention of his predecessor's name. 'I see.' His voice was suddenly steely and determined. 'Well, Luqiao isn't here anymore.' The Secretary put his hands on his hips. 'The vehicle I have been given is a government vehicle for official matters, not private use.' He sighed heavily. 'I'm sorry, Shaozhen, but Secretary Lam and the Party are putting me under a lot of pressure. I haven't even been able to get funds to repair the school window.'

Shaozhen swallowed. 'Is it because of your plans to build the new Hongsha? Is that why you've been going into town so much?'

Xian sighed. 'It's not that simple, I'm afraid. The Party system is complicated and there are many, many considerations beyond Hongsha and the township.' He shook his head. 'In the end, I just have to do what they say.'

'But you're the Secretary!' Shaozhen heard his voice rising. 'Surely you know what's best for the village? That's why you're in charge!'

The Secretary shook his head. Shaozhen realised that Xian looked much older than at the time they had first met.

'It's not quite that easy. Even as the Village Secretary, I don't get much of a say in the village matters. That's reserved for the more senior officials, above even Secretary Lam. The rest of us are just expected to hand down orders.'

'But you have all those great ideas…'

'In time, Shaozhen. In time. But for now, they're watching my every move.' Xian was practically whispering. 'Everything I do is being scrutinised. One wrong step and…' He shook his head. 'Anyway, that's why I can't lend you the truck. I can't sanction the use of a government vehicle for private matters.'

Shaozhen felt the blood drain from his face when he realised Xian wasn't going to change his mind.

Without the truck, how was he going to get Nainai to the hospital?

But then Xian's expression softened. 'But look, just because I can't help you as the Village Secretary, it doesn't mean I can't help you as Hongsha villager Xian. Come on.' He stepped outside and waved for Shaozhen to follow.

Xian led him past the truck towards an untended piece of land. Shaozhen peered between the overgrown weeds, and saw there was a vehicle hidden there: an old moped with small wheels, an even tinier engine, and a wide trailer attached to the back. *A farmer's sanlun motorcycle.*

Xian placed both hands on the handlebars and beamed. He looked younger standing beside the trike, like a schoolboy. 'This is my own personal vehicle from back in the days when I was still a student. We loaded fifteen pigs onto the back once!' He had a wistful look on his face. 'Petrol is expensive, so I prefer to use the pushbike. But it's the most utilitarian vehicle around and I'm happy to take your nainai to the hospital on this myself.'

Shaozhen was speechless. He stared at the trike. How were they going to carry his injured grandmother all the way to Xifeng?

Fourteen

The engine sputtered to life like a wheezing dog. Xian nodded for Shaozhen to get on the back, and he perched uneasily on the tiny seat, putting his arms around the Secretary's waist. Shaozhen had never been on the back of any motorbike before.

Xian took off and Shaozhen felt his heart jolt and a prickling along his spinal column. The path into the centre of the village was narrow and bumpy but Xian ratcheted the trike down the rocks, the engine straining under the weight of two bodies.

They sped down the road, past the withered vegetable gardens. Finally, Xian pulled up at the Lu house. A few of the villagers had gathered out the front but they all made way when they saw the Village Secretary storming up to the door.

Nainai, Yangyang and the doctor were still inside Shaozhen's bedroom.

'Greetings, Wang Daifu.' Xian gave a deep bow that caught the doctor off guard.

'Secretary Xian, I didn't realise that you would be coming.'

The Secretary smiled too bright and too broadly, a politician's smile. 'I'm a member of this village now. I intend to contribute as any other villager would. No need to treat me any differently to the rest.'

'That's an interesting statement, Secretary, with your extended absence to the village you belong to,' Wang Daifu replied.

'I – I…' Xian turned bright red, caught off guard by the doctor's remark.

Wang Daifu quirked an eyebrow. Over the past few weeks Shaozhen had seen the same accusing glares directed at Xian from other villagers. He couldn't help feeling sorry for the young Secretary.

'Secretary, you said we can take my grandmother to the hospital on your trike?' Shaozhen asked, hoping to divert Xian's attention.

'Of – of course,' Xian stammered. He stooped over Nainai, who was still lying on the floor moaning softly. They had made her as comfortable as they could with a pillow for her head, and Yangyang was still pressing the wet cloth to her cheek. 'Shaozhen, we'll need to lift her into the back of the trike.' He nodded towards Yangyang. 'You must be Shaozhen's sister. Can you fetch us some blankets?' Yangyang rushed to obey. Neither she nor Shaozhen felt the need to correct Xian's mistake.

Yangyang found two bedsheets and Xian instructed her to tie them together. Nainai was too hurt to stand up, so they carefully manoeuvred her onto the sheet. They grabbed a corner each and lifted the old woman up in a makeshift sling. Nainai cried out in pain but they kept her steady and carried her outside.

Xian managed to open the tray at the back of his trike without dropping his corner of the sheet. The four of them gently set Nainai in the middle of the trailer bed. Yangyang ran back into the house and found more bedding and pillows to jam in, creating a nest in the trailer. They tucked the sheets in around her like a rice noodle roll.

'You can get in the back,' Xian said to the group. 'I won't go very fast. I promise.'

Wang Daifu sat behind Xian, while Shaozhen and Yangyang squished in with Nainai on the trike's trailer, taking extra care not to bump into the bundle of blankets that was their grandmother. After experiencing Xian barrel down the road on the bike like an out-of-control rabbit, Shaozhen was worried. But Xian, true to his word, set a slow and steady pace.

On the bike, the trip to town was much quicker than the daily walk, but it still felt like an effort. Shaozhen imagined breaking down by the side of the road, but the engine chugged on.

Their progress stalled when they got to the outskirts of Xifeng and were caught in the queue of bicycles, hand-pulled trolleys and the occasional motorbike. Another water line was forming, but it would be hours before a new truck would arrive.

'Move along. Come on,' Wang Daifu shouted to the crowd, among other things, his language expletive enough to make Shaozhen blush. He was stunned to see this side of the usually gentle old doctor.

Finally, they reached the Xifeng Hospital, a two-storey building on the other side of the town. Xian pulled up at the wide empty parking bay out the front. Wang Daifu hopped off while the Secretary was still turning off the engine.

A tiny figure clad in pink coveralls and a face mask rushed outside to greet them.

'Nurse, I'm Secretary Xian,' he barked in an authoritative voice. 'This woman is hurt and needs immediate care.'

But the nurse didn't pay him any attention. Instead, she turned to the doctor. 'Wang Yisheng, what brings you here?'

'Nurse Jin, it's good to see you. I hope your children are well.' Wang Daifu bowed deeply.

'It's good to see you, Wang Yisheng. What do we have here?'

'The old woman has fallen and possibly broken her hip,' he said. 'She needs urgent attention. I'll be staying on to look after her myself.' Nurse Jin nodded and hurried back inside for assistance.

Xian looked embarrassed. He stood awkwardly in the parking lot as the hospital staff rushed to help Nainai out of the trike and onto a stretcher.

As they pushed her towards the hospital entrance, Shaozhen paused and then ran back to the Secretary. 'Thank you for your help.'

Xian's whole face broke into a smile, and he once

again reminded Shaozhen of a schoolboy. 'Of course, you're welcome. Please let me know if there's anything more I can do.'

He revved the engine of the trike and puttered off.

Shaozhen hurried through the double doors into the hospital.

◉◉◉

Nurse Jin made Shaozhen and Yangyang wait in the hall. There were only two plastic chairs, both taken, so they had to stand. Shaozhen tried to distract himself by counting the black and grey tiles on the hallway floor. He had counted seventy-seven black tiles and was up to one hundred and eighty-two white tiles when Nurse Jin came over.

'You can see her now, but be careful. She mustn't be moved.'

Nainai was lying on one of the beds with a drip stuck into her arm. A second nurse was hanging a clear plastic bag of fluid on a stand beside her bed. Her head was cradled by a thin pillow that looked like a lumpy chunjuan, spring roll, her eyes half-closed.

Nainai couldn't lift her head, but she smiled when she saw her grandson approach. He knelt next to the flimsy metal bedframe and took her hand, careful not to grip it too tightly. The mattress springs beneath her squeaked when she moved.

'Shaozhen, look at your silly old grandmother.' Her fingers were long and thin, her skin as translucent as rice paper so that he could see the thick veins underneath. 'What a mess I've made.'

'No, Nainai. I'm sorry. I should have been looking after you more. Helped more on the fields.' Shaozhen shut his eyes to keep the tears at bay. 'I promise to be a dutiful grandson and to take better care of you, Nainai, no matter what.'

She squeezed his hand, trembling with the effort. 'My dear grandson. You are a good boy. Your parents would be very proud of you.'

Shaozhen's heart twisted at the mention of his parents. Right now, more than anything, he wished that Ma was here. 'I'll try to call Ba, let him know what happened.'

But Nainai shook her head. 'Hush. Don't mention it to your parents. There's no need, I don't want them to worry.'

'But—'

'Their hours are long. Your parents need to focus on their work.'

'Laobo.' Yangyang was hurrying over, clutching a single bottle of water to her chest. 'The doctors said this was their last bottle. A new shipment doesn't arrive until tomorrow.'

'Oh, child.' Nainai clutched Yangyang's hand, her eyes misty. 'You are so good to me, but you should keep the water for yourself.' Yangyang opened her mouth to protest but Nainai shook her head. 'Now, I think I've been lying around long enough. We have to get back. Shaozhen, Yangyang, help me up.' She tried to push herself up onto her elbows, straining from the effort.

Yangyang gasped.

'Ah, Po, Grandmother, you can't be getting up.' Nurse Jin came over to scold his grandmother. 'You can't put any weight on that hip or you'll be paralysed for the rest of your life.'

'Nonsense.' Nainai was trying to get up, but she was struggling to even lift her head off the pillow. 'There's no time to be lying about. I need to look after the farm.'

'Po, please.' Nurse Jin laid a gentle but firm hand on Nainai's shoulder. She fell back, the springs beneath the mattress squeaking.

'You're going to have to stay in the hospital for a while,' Nurse Jin said. 'Wang Yisheng said you could have broken a hip. You can't be moving around or you'll snap in two.'

'But I have to get back. The children...'

'Don't worry about us, Nainai.' Shaozhen stood up. 'We'll look after ourselves. I promise.' He glanced at Yangyang and she nodded. 'You just focus on getting better and coming home.'

Her eyes glistened. 'But Shaozhen...'

Shaozhen leant over and stroked his grandmother on the cheek. 'Please, Nainai. You have to get better.' He forced back a sob but he couldn't stop the wavering in his voice. 'You can't leave me like Ma and Ba.'

A single tear emerged near the bridge of Nainai's nose. 'You are more and more like your father every day.'

Shaozhen and Yangyang stayed at Nainai's bedside until the nurses told them they had to go home. The sun was setting over the Song Mountains and the road was deserted as they made their way back to the village.

Yangyang was quiet on the walk. Shaozhen thought nothing of it until he heard strangled whimpers. Her head was bent towards the road.

'Yangyang? Are you okay?'

She looked up and Shaozhen saw glistening trails running down her cheeks. Her mouth was twisted into an ugly crescent, a strand of hair stuck to her lips. She let out a loud wail. 'Laobo!'

'Yangyang, it's all right.' Shaozhen reached out to grip her shoulder, his hand stiff and unsure. He had never seen Yangyang crying before. Even when she had first arrived at their house after her grandmother died, she hadn't shed a single tear.

She grabbed him suddenly and hugged him fiercely, sobbing into his shoulder. 'What if she doesn't make it back? What if she never comes home?'

'Hey, don't worry. Nainai will be home before you know it.' He patted her on the back. 'Wang Daifu's the best doctor in the township. She's in good hands.'

Yangyang kept wailing. Finally, she pulled away, dragging the back of her hand across her eyes. Her cheeks were bright red and she sniffed loudly. She didn't say anything else to him, just turned and continued their walk home. But as they approached the entrance to Hongsha, she spun around and faced Shaozhen. 'My waipo, grandmother, started off with a simple fever. It went on for two days. On the third day, I thought she was getting better, but in the middle of the night she started shaking and couldn't stop. By the time we got her to the hospital, her skin was too hot to touch. She was gone the next day.' Yangyang's bottom lip quivered.

Shaozhen swallowed and licked his dry lips. 'I'm – I'm sorry.' He didn't know what else to say.

'I just don't want the same thing to happen to your nainai.'

I don't either. He left it unsaid.

When they arrived home, Shaozhen found a letter addressed to him, shoved under the door. He left Yangyang to prepare dinner and went into his room. Shaozhen held the envelope in his hands, recognising his mother's hand. Her writing was neat, though some of the letters looked blockier than they were supposed to be – his mother and father hadn't finished more than four years of primary school each. It was the first time she had written since she had left for Guangzhou. It seemed like a lifetime ago.

The thinness of the envelope was surprising. He knew that his father was always busy, but he thought his mother at least would send a present: a magazine or some clothes, something she thought her son would like from the city. Shaozhen was still hopeful as he tore open the packet.

He unfolded the single sheet of almost translucent paper.

Shaozhen,
   How are you? Your father and I are working hard. The factory was very busy this month. We had to redo

a shipment from a previous order. The seller said the quality was not good. Your father has not slept. His supervisor has been hard and said they will dock the pay of the workers who do not stay overtime to fix the problem.

I hope you are looking after Nainai and being a good helper. The city has water restrictions because of the lack of rain. This means the water bill has been higher than our rent. Ba says that we cannot send money. Next month, we will send extra. You are a good boy. We miss you every day.

Take care of your nainai. She is getting older and we are so worried but we know she has a strong heart. She will look after you. You make us all so proud.

Thank you for your letter. I am so happy to hear that you passed your exams and that your teacher was impressed with your marks. I am so very proud of you. We are hoping that with a good harvest, maybe you will have the money to join us in the city for senior school. Nothing would make us happier than to have you by our side.

We love you so much, our precious son.

Your loving parents,

Ma and Ba

Shaozhen read the letter again, a tear stinging the corner of his eye. There was no money. His parents were relying on the income from a bountiful harvest to put him through school, but the crops were all shrivelled and dying. There would be no senior school for him. No university. Without the harvest, they might even starve.

And his parents didn't even know that Nainai was in hospital.

He recalled Nainai's instructions. *I don't want them to worry. Your parents need to focus on their work.*

He looked up when he heard a gentle knocking. Yangyang was standing by his doorway. 'I couldn't find much to make—' She stopped when she saw Shaozhen's face. 'Is everything okay?' Her eyes went to the letter.

He nodded, not trusting his own voice, and tucked the letter into his shirt.

'Are you hungry?' Yangyang held up some scrawny cabbage leaves. 'I can make dinner.'

Shaozhen swallowed the lump in his throat and shook his head.

It was dark outside already and they went about the house in silence. They cleaned up the mess from that morning and then turned on the television. There was no basketball on, so they watched a silly game show instead. Neither said a word. Without Nainai's soft humming and presence the house felt empty. Cold.

At the end of the program, Yangyang went to her room and shut the door without even saying goodnight. Shaozhen sat, bathed in the white glow of the television, completely alone.

Fifteen

Shaozhen tossed and turned through the night. The letter from Ma, Yangyang's story about her waipo, and seeing Nainai so weak and frail had all left a feeling of uneasiness. His mind was hazy, and he felt like his body belonged to someone else, or some part of it was missing.

He dozed and then got up, shuffling towards the door with bare feet. He retrieved the two buckets and the bamboo pole from where they were kept at the side of the house and set off down the tree-lined path.

It was too early even for the birds, but he made his way through the village to the road by moonlight.

When he arrived at Xifeng, he was surprised to find a few villagers already waiting with their buckets in the dim light of the early morning He walked past them to the other end of the town, barely making a sound as he padded down the pavement.

The hospital doors were locked from the inside. Shaozhen pressed his face against the window but thick

128

curtains blocked his view. He went around the building to where he thought the nurse's office was located and rapped on the glass a few times.

A young face appeared, framed by dark hair and a prim nurse's cap. Shaozhen mimed going inside, pressing his palms together to plead his case, but the nurse just shook her head and disappeared.

There was nothing else he could do, so Shaozhen went back to the water queue with his buckets. He nodded to a grey-haired man picking his teeth at the front of the queue and found a spot to wait not too far from the road near a row of food stalls. The delicious smell of steaming meat pancakes caught his attention and his stomach growled. He hadn't really eaten at all yesterday nor this morning, and he was feeling a bit faint. He sat down and hugged his legs. What he wouldn't give to have just a taste of a fresh roujiamo, piping hot and fluffy!

His stomach grumbled again but he tried to ignore it. His parents couldn't send money. There was certainly no money for snacks, especially not with Nainai in hospital and the extra costs of medicine.

He sniffed once, twice, and then broke down sobbing.

'Wah, are you kidding me? Big boy crying in the street?' The stern voice sounded familiar. Shaozhen looked up. It was the old man from the hut in the mountains, the one who had found Xiaoping. Shen Yeye, the little boy had called him. *What's he doing here?*

He was leaning on his cane, a small bucket clutched in his other hand. Since he had no teeth, his lips folded over his gums, but Shaozhen knew that he was frowning.

'I'm…I'm sorry.' Shaozhen felt like he should be afraid of this man but his emotions were in turmoil. He snivelled and wiped his nose with the back of his hand.

Old man Shen set down his bucket and reached into his faded cotton shirt, his hands shaking. He pulled out a grey handkerchief and handed it to Shaozhen. 'Boys don't cry in the middle of the street. Only babies. Okay?'

Despite the harshness of his words, Shaozhen felt strangely comforted. He nodded, then blew his nose hard.

Shen took the handkerchief back without blinking and reached into his pocket again. He pulled out a single crumpled note. 'Go get an old man some of those roujiamo over there. Don't let her try to short-change you. That's enough for two and she knows it.'

Shaozhen took the money without a word. He raced over to the stall owner and offered the note. She gave him the once-over, eyeing his bare feet and stiff, grubby clothes. But then she handed him a steaming hot parcel, with two roujiamo tucked inside.

Shaozhen stared at the food in his palm, trying not to drool as he carried the roujiamo back to the old man.

Shen reached for the pack and extracted a warm roujiamo before handing Shaozhen the other. 'Eat,' he commanded. 'No more tears. Unbecoming.'

'Thank – thank you, Mr Shen.'

Shen scoffed and waved his pancake. 'That's the other thing with boys these days. These ridiculous manners, like we still live under imperial rule.'

Shaozhen took the roujiamo from the packet. He couldn't remember the last time he had bought anything from a food stall. Ma and Nainai said it was a waste of money. The roujiamo was no bigger than an egg, and a small one at that. He pulled the white bread apart, watching the steam emerge from inside like a blossom, revealing the hot sticky pork in its centre. He pinched the bun and took a bite. The sweetness hit his tastebuds like a tidal wave, a flood of sticky pleasure and happiness. He hadn't had a treat like this since the New Year and he was careful to savour the first mouthful, taking the time to let the sinews of braised meat melt on his tongue before swallowing.

He glanced at Shen. The old man was munching away, the soft bread emulsifying between his flapping gums. 'Before the drought, I could keep the dough to make my own soft bread at home. But you have to keep feeding it.' Shen shook his head. 'I miss my bread. Everything else is hard and tasteless as rocks.'

More people were arriving now, and the queue was starting to form. Shaozhen finished his roujiamo, his stomach warm and nourished. He picked up his pole and then took the old man's bucket.

'Mr Shen, I'll line up for the water. You can wait here.'

'Hah, are you kidding me? You think I would let that bucket out of my sight?' But he stayed put and Shaozhen joined the fray, feeling Shen's eyes fixed on him.

The first truck arrived and he was one of the first to receive water. It was pure and fresh, and Shaozhen wondered whether this was why Shen had been out here before the others.

'Hey, two buckets per household. You know the rules,' the driver barked when Shaozhen put down Shen's bucket.

'It's not for me, it's for Mr Shen.' He nodded towards the old man, squatting by the kerb. 'Please, he's been waiting for a long time and I wanted to help him.'

The driver hesitated and Shaozhen heard some grumbling from behind him but eventually he relented and held Shen's bucket under the stream.

They walked back along the road to Hongsha in silence, Shaozhen carrying both of his own buckets on the pole, as well as Shen's small pail. The going was slow, and Shen stopped to rest twice, mopping the sweat from his brow with the dirty handkerchief.

He stopped again to lean heavily against a tree, his whole body sagging. 'Am I holding you back, boy? You don't have to wait. I can take care of myself, you know. No matter what anyone says, I'm not a kooky old man.'

'No, no, of course not, Mr Shen,' Shaozhen said.

An awkward silence fell over them and Shaozhen tried to think of something to talk about. Shen seemed mean on the surface, but he'd bought roujiamo, plus Xiaoping seemed to like him. Shaozhen wondered if Shen had any family. 'Do your children live with you in the mountain, Mr Shen?'

The old man's face darkened. 'All right, enough with this "Mr Shen" business as well. Call me Shugong.'

'Okay…Great Uncle Shen.' Shaozhen smiled, hoping

the expression would be returned. He received a grunt and a nod instead.

When the pair started walking again, the only sound was the creaking of the bamboo strips that held the buckets to the pole. But then they were interrupted by a soft *chip chip chirrup.*

A small brown bird landed on the edge of one of the buckets, the surprise of it nearly throwing Shaozhen off balance. A young maque. Its feathers were surprisingly glossy, its eyes shining and bright. The creature cocked its head to the side and stared up at him, then dropped forwards like it was bowing deeply.

'Maque. Nuisance birds.' Shen shook his head. 'Our generation spent a season trying to get rid of these pests. The Great Sparrow Campaign.' He hoisted his walking stick in the air. 'We shouted and blew trumpets and beat the drums until the maque fell out of the sky from sheer exhaustion.'

Shaozhen reached his hand out to the maque and whistled. The bird was curious, eyeing the small perch he'd made with his forefinger. Finally, it hopped on. Its claws were thin but not too sharp, and Shaozhen lowered the little creature towards the surface of the water.

The bird bent down and drank.

'Wasting water, giving it to some pest.' Shen's remark was laced with disapproval but Shaozhen didn't care. He smiled as the bird dipped its teeny beak back to the liquid, stretching its soft wings as it tried to keep its balance.

'You young ones are all softies. I'd bet you'd keep it as a pet.'

Shaozhen shook his head. 'My father had pet birds, but I didn't like seeing them in the cage, so I set them free. Do your children like animals?'

'I don't have children,' Shen spat, his eyebrows pulling forwards like little spears. Shaozhen felt his face reddening. He hadn't meant to offend Shen. But then the wrinkled features softened. 'I lost my boys to the big famine. The littlest was three and he died in my arms.'

Shaozhen knew only vague details about the big famine and the history of that time. Three years of hardship, bitterness and misfortune had befallen the country between 1959 and 1961, and many people had died. He'd been taught in school that they called them 'Three Bitter Years'. He'd asked Nainai about it – she would have been a girl then, just twelve or thirteen. But while Nainai was always happy to regale him with stories about how tough her life had been, she never gave specific details. 'We all starved as children,' she'd say. 'The Chinese people have suffered many hardships but we have persevered.'

'What happened to him? Your son.' Shaozhen knew he shouldn't ask but his curiosity was piqued.

'What happened to any of us?' Shen's eyes were moist. 'Dark times had befallen us. There was no more food. We'd eaten it all. Everything we grew on the fields was controlled by the cadres. They sent it all away, every last bit, and all we were left with was soil and rocks.' His voice was so quiet that Shaozhen strained to hear him. 'Their ma went first, she got sick and there was no medicine. I tried to feed the boys enough. I would have eaten nothing, as long as the boys could. But there was no food to put in their bowls. My elder son was climbing a tree, hoping the nest he spotted would have eggs in it. He fell and hit his head, died on the spot.

'My littlest one, he was so strong. He was his ma's darling, his eyes big and shining like a little bird. That's what she called him, her little bird. He hardly ate anything – he was so tiny – but even that amount I couldn't provide.'

Shaozhen felt his heart wrench. He wasn't aware of just how hard it had been in the village for old men like Great Uncle Shen and his own grandparents. 'I'm sorry, Shugong.'

The old man had his face in his hands. His body shook like he was crying, but when he looked up at Shaozhen, his face was dry. 'Sorry doesn't erase sorrow. But let me tell you something, boy: after all that, you learn to rely on yourself. You learn to find your own strength, carry your own water.' He nodded to the buckets. 'You learn what it takes to survive. You don't depend on anyone, certainly not the local officials, you hear?'

The maque chirped loudly, as if to agree. It flapped its wings and took off.

'Not even a nod of thanks,' Shen grumbled. 'Nothing but pests.'

Sixteen

Shaozhen and Shen arrived at the fork in the road. The sun was climbing swiftly towards its peak. Shaozhen could feel his shirt plastered to his back and Shen was wiping sweat from his brow with his handkerchief. Suddenly Shaozhen had an idea.

'It's this way to the village, Shugong. Come with me,' Shaozhen said, pointing. 'Everyone has been wanting to meet the old man who saved Xiaoping. Then I can help you take the water home.'

Shen bristled, his hunched back straightening as much as it could. 'What do you take me for? An invalid?'

Shaozhen was taken aback. 'I – I just meant that I could help you carry it. I didn't mean to offend you.'

'You villagers always think you're better than me.' Shen was shouting now, his whole demeanour transformed. 'I didn't ask for your help, did I? I've managed fine on my own for years. Meanwhile, you lot can't even keep track of a three-year-old boy.' Shen's whole body was trembling and his cane wobbled violently as if it was possessed.

'Great Uncle, please, I didn't mean anything by it.'
Why is Shen so afraid of the village?

'Don't "Great Uncle" me anymore, boy.' Spit was shooting from Shen's lips. 'I'm nobody to you or anyone else and I'm happy that way.'

And before Shaozhen could say anything else, the old man reached out his knobby hand like a claw and snatched the bucket from Shaozhen's grasp. He stormed away, moving faster than he had their entire walk back.

Shaozhen stood there, the weight of the buckets on the pole digging into his neck, torn between running after Shen and letting him go.

The old man headed up the path towards the mountain. Going after him would mean leaving Shaozhen's water haul behind: there wasn't any way he could make the climb with all that weight swinging from his bamboo pole. And Shen was quite clear about not wanting to have anything to do with the village; it was probably best to leave him be.

Shaozhen walked through the village, his mind clouded with questions. What had happened to Shen? The man had talked about his difficult past and his sons' passing. The story had broken Shaozhen's heart in two but he was sure there was something else. He'd seen the fear and rage in the man's eyes at the mere mention of the village.

'Shaozhen.' Aunty Wu was sweeping her stoop as he emerged from the tree-lined path. 'How's your nainai? Is she still in the hospital?'

Shaozhen placed his buckets on the ground. 'They wouldn't let me see her. I'm going to go back this afternoon.' He rolled his shoulders one at time, relieved to be free of the weight. He took in Aunty Wu's limp white perm and hunched-over form. She looked drained and tired, a far cry from her usual lively self. The drought had taken its toll on even the most steadfast and resilient villagers. He was suddenly curious. 'Aunty Wu, how long have you lived in the village?'

She looked up. 'All my life, child. Would you believe, I was born in this very house? And my hope is that when it's my time to go, I will pass peacefully within its walls.'

'What happened during the famine? The Three Bitter Years?'

Aunty Wu narrowed her eyes. 'What do you know about the Three Bitter Years, Shaozhen?'

He shrugged. 'Not much. But a lot of people died. There was no food, people were eating bark and wild plants and things. In school, I learned it was because of natural disasters, but old Shen said—'

'Old Shen?' Her eyes shot open, wide and round. 'Where have you been talking to that old kook?'

Shaozhen felt the blood rising to his face. 'I saw him in Xifeng. He was lining up for water.'

Aunty Wu *tsk*ed loudly. 'First Xiaoping, now you. What garbage has he been filling your mind with?'

'I – he just mentioned the famine. That things were hard and he lost his sons and wife. I didn't realise it had been so bad.'

138

She hesitated before answering. 'To be honest, I was just a baby then so I don't remember much. But I know that we all suffered during that time. Even so, Shen was a different kind, cut from a different mould. I was still a child when I heard about the strange man living in the mountains.'

'Why does he live alone up there?'

'Let me make one thing clear: he chose to. Nobody drove him out, no matter what he says. But if he didn't want to be a part of the village, then it's better that he left.' Her eyes were fierce and she lifted her chin. 'And that's fine by me.' Aunty Wu picked up her broom and stormed into her house.

Her words left Shaozhen more confused than ever. It was the second time that morning he was left standing on his own, completely befuddled.

●●●

Shaozhen emptied his load into the sealed containers they were using for storage, then filled one of the buckets partway with recycled water to take out to the fields. Despite the drought, he and Yangyang were determined to save whatever part of the harvest they could.

Yangyang was already there, digging troughs along the rows of withered corn. She worked quickly and methodically as always, her sharp voice cutting through the whistling of the dry leaves as she dragged the hoe through the lines of crops. 'Hyah. Hyah. Hyah.' Today he thought she sounded more like a heroine from an action movie than a banshee. She stopped when she spotted him, using her hand to shield her face from the sun.

'Nice of you to show up.' She threw her tools on the ground, taking care not to squash the plants.

Shaozhen smiled. Despite their more tender exchanges lately, her tongue still cracked like a whip. But, more and more, Shaozhen was realising her toughness was a front and inside she was concerned and caring. He held up his bucket as a peace offering.

Her harsh glower relaxed. 'Did you visit Laobo?'

Shaozhen shook his head, then wiped the sweat from his brow. 'They wouldn't let me in. We should try later.' He set down the bucket and surveyed the crops around him. He struggled to recall the information Nainai had tried to drill into him about farming. 'I was thinking we should pull out the plants and check the roots. Get rid of the ones that are long dead, focus on the ones worth saving. We might even be able to water them.'

Yangyang snorted. 'Oh, the big basketball star thinks he's a farmer now.'

'It's a good idea and you know it.' Shaozhen was rewarded with a sly smirk. He stooped over and dug around the roots of one of the plants with his fingers. He felt something snapping as he tried to wedge his hand under to extract the plant from the earth.

'It's not looking good,' Yangyang said, peering over his shoulder at the scraggly tangle of skinny roots that he'd pulled out. She knelt down and pulled out another plant. It was just as sickly. They drew up plant after plant, their hopes cast aside with the growing pile of lifeless vegetation.

Shaozhen peered down at yet another snarl of parched roots, ready to cast it to the ground. But then something caught his eye. He squinted. 'Wait! Look, this one's still alive.' He pulled out a single white strand and grinned in triumph.

Yangyang examined the plant. Sure enough, that one white root was thick and glossy, a healthy specimen among its ghastly neighbours. She nodded and Shaozhen caught the wisp of a smile.

'It's so tiny and delicate,' Yangyang said. 'Like the roots of chrysanthemums.'

Shaozhen snorted. 'Wah, listen to the peasant girl trying to speak poetry.'

'Hmmph.' She twirled the end of her plait between her fingers. 'I just like chrysanthemums. They're sweet-smelling and can be used for tea.'

Shaozhen smiled and the pair went to work, pulling away the dead fibres to save that single root that tied the plant to life. 'It's not all bad. We find enough of these, then move them to a smaller patch and care for that. If we're lucky, we might even save a quarter of the harvest.' His spirits lifted and he felt better than he had in days. He flashed Yangyang a cocky grin. He was surprised that the two of them made a good team.

They were halfway up the field when they heard a strange whirring from the road. 'What's that?' Yangyang stood up, using her hand to block the sun.

Shaozhen recognised the sound straightaway. *An engine*. But it was too weak and tinny to be a car or even the Secretary's trike. The object approaching them was lumpy and small. As it came into view and he realised who it was, Shaozhen let out a whoop and a holler.

The little moped sounded more like a mosquito than one of the fancy Japanese Kawasakis in the movies, but to Shaozhen it made no difference.

'The motorcycle! You fixed it!'

Chun pulled the moped to a stop beside them. 'What do you think?' he said with a grin.

Shaozhen could feel his lips pulling apart into the biggest smile. He trailed his hands over the handlebars and stooped down to peer at the engine. 'Amazing!' he said, not trying to hide his awe. 'Can I drive it?'

Chun frowned. 'I don't know if that's a good idea. I mean, it's a bit finicky…'

Shaozhen was embarrassed he'd asked, realising just how much the bike would mean to his friend. It would be like giving away a prized possession. 'Well, can you give me a ride then?'

Chun smiled and nodded. Yangyang scoffed loudly, but she was staring at the bike, her eyes wide and round. Shaozhen climbed onto the back of the bike and put his arms around the other boy's waist. 'Hang on tight.'

The bike took off. Shaozhen whooped again. It felt different to riding Xian's trike when he had felt at first in fear for his life, and so worried for Nainai. They wouldn't have been going any faster than ten or maybe fifteen kilometres per hour according to the little speedometer that Chun pointed out to him but he felt like they were racing the F1. He spread his arms out like wings, tilting his face to the sky. The sun beamed down on him while their movement through the air formed a cool breeze, pushing against his short-cropped hair.

A sudden, sharp turn made Shaozhen cry out in surprise and clutch at the seat behind him. Chun laughed, tilting the bike towards the dirt as he leant in. Shaozhen was amazed at how expertly Chun handled the machine, like he'd been riding motorcycles all his life, instead of just tinkering with the broken scrap heap that had only roared to life this morning.

Finally, Chun turned the bike around and they headed back to the fields. Chun idled the bike and let Shaozhen hop off.

'What do you think?' Chun asked.

Shaozhen couldn't stop smiling. 'That was incredible. I can't believe you got it to work. You're a genius!'

Chun shrugged and stared at the ground, trying to deflect his friend's gushing praise.

Yangyang was working near the edge of the field, when Chun suddenly called, 'Yangyang! Do you want a ride?'

She glanced behind her, as if looking for someone else, then turned back to Chun. 'Me?' Chun nodded and motioned for her to hop on. Shaozhen was amused that she had no spiteful words for them. After everything they'd been through with Nainai in the hospital and working side by side these past few days, they'd grown much closer. He would almost call her his friend.

'Well, come on,' Chun said.

Yangyang hurried over. She was taller than Chun, so she had to hunch down quite a bit as she awkwardly put her arms around the boy. When she was finally seated, Chun took off again.

All through her ride, Shaozhen could tell that Yangyang was laughing, her plait undone, her cheeks rosy and flushed and her eyes shining.

'Thank you, Chun!' Yangyang said as she climbed off the back of the bike. She beamed at Shaozhen. 'Wow. That was so fun!'

Shaozhen was certain he had never heard Yangyang say the word *fun* before. She smiled again and, for a second, Shaozhen thought she might even pass for pretty but he quickly pushed *that* thought out of his head.

Seventeen

Shaozhen and Yangyang visited Nainai in the hospital in the afternoon, but she was asleep so she missed their visit. They returned the following morning, but Nurse Jin made them wait in the hallway again.

Finally, Wang Daifu came out to see them. 'I have an update on your nainai's condition,' he said. 'After a thorough examination, I have concluded that Nainai's fainting spells were the result of stress and dehydration. The good news is I believe that her hip may only be badly bruised from the fall, not broken.'

'That's great news,' Shaozhen cried, but the doctor frowned.

'However, without an X-ray it's impossible to tell. I would like to send her to the city, for X-rays and possibly a surgical procedure.'

Shaozhen was stunned. If they sent Nainai to the city, then he would be entirely alone.

'But we could never afford that,' Yangyang cried in dismay. This was also true. Hospitals in the city cost a lot of money if you weren't a local resident. This was part of the system of hukou. 'Isn't there anything more you can do?'

Wang Daifu let out a weary sigh. 'The only thing I can recommend is that we keep a strict eye on it. I can give her some herbs to ease the pain. She must stay in bed. No work of any kind,' he warned.

Shaozhen and Yangyang promised the doctor they would follow his instructions.

Meanwhile, Nainai had been trying to insist that she was ready to go home so she was thrilled to hear that Wang Daifu had finally agreed. 'About time! What a waste, letting me rot here in this godforsaken hospital. I'll be a corpse in no time if they keep me here any longer.' Shaozhen winced at the crassness of her remarks; he hoped the kindly nurses hadn't heard her!

Shaozhen had wanted to ask Secretary Xian if they could use his trike again, but Xian hadn't been seen for days. The rumour was that he was staying in town, working on 'secret Party business' with Secretary Lam. 'Just another Luqiao in sheep's clothing,' Aunty Law had remarked. Shaozhen wanted to stand up for Xian, but he couldn't find the right words. *Can Xian really change things?*

Chun had offered to take Nainai home on the back of his restored moped, but Shaozhen doubted his grandmother would agree to the suggestion.

'We'll have to wheel her back in a barrow, like the pigs,' Yangyang said finally.

They went to find Kang to see if his grandfather would lend them one of the shiny wheelbarrows from the shop. But the shop was shut and Kang was nowhere to be found. Finally, they managed to borrow an old one from Chun's grandfather, who made Shaozhen promise fifty times not to put a ding or dent in it.

A nurse was pushing Nainai out in the wheelchair as they pulled it up to the hospital entrance.

'Wah, these children have lost their minds!' Nainai shouted. 'They think I'm a pig for slaughter.' She struggled to get out of the wheelchair. 'Forget this, give me a cane. I can walk home. I'm not livestock. What if the villagers see me?'

'Nainai, we don't want you to hurt yourself,' Shaozhen pleaded. 'It's the only way. Wang Daifu said you have to be secured and you can't put any weight on your hip.'

Nainai looked helplessly at the nurse, who shrugged. She glared at her grandson and adoptive granddaughter, her eyes like poison darts that made Shaozhen's skin prickle. 'Fine,' she spat. The nurse slid her hand under Nainai's armpit to lift her up but her patient slapped it away. 'I don't need help.'

But in the end, it took all three of them to manoeuvre Nainai out of the wheelchair and into the blanket and pillow-lined wheelbarrow. Yangyang tucked a thick floral-pattered doona around her, and then she was stuffed in tight, like a bulging sausage.

Yangyang and Shaozhen each picked up one handle of the wheelbarrow and proceeded down the road.

Fortunately, the water truck had left and most of the villagers had gone home. Shaozhen was certain Nainai would not take fondly to being paraded past their neighbours in such a fashion.

'Come on now – faster! I don't want anyone to see me like this,' Nainai scolded.

The going was slow and despite Nainai's protests, they had to stop and rest. It was late in the afternoon and the sun was baking hot.

Nainai had grown quiet now, her eyes shut and her head lolling. Yangyang laid a hand across her forehead. 'She's clammy but not sweating.' She pulled back the blankets. Without them, Nainai looked so small; she barely filled up the wheelbarrow.

Shaozhen bit his lip. 'Wang Daifu said we have to keep her hydrated. Do you have any water?'

The girl shook her head but then her face brightened. 'Look over there.' She pointed down the road. There was a man leading a donkey and cart. The back of the cart was full of plastic-wrapped pallets of bottled water.

'Sir! Sir!' Yangyang waved her arms wildly, trying to flag him down. 'Water, sir. How much to buy one bottle of water for our grandmother? She is unwell and going to faint from the sun.' She reached into her shirt where Shaozhen knew she kept pocket money from her parents.

The man slowed beside them, yanking at the donkey's halter. He narrowed his eyes. The expression on his face was something between a smile and a sneer, and his cheeks were flushed from the heat.

'Bottle of water? One hundred yuan.'

Shaozhen felt his mouth fall open with shock. A hundred yuan was more than he paid for a month's worth of meat. It was almost a quarter of the money that Ba had been sending them every month. *A hundred yuan for a bottle?*

'You're crazy,' Yangyang cried, withdrawing her hand. 'How can one bottle of water cost one hundred yuan?'

The man smirked, his eyes fixed on Yangyang. 'Haven't you heard, little miss? There's a drought. Supply and demand, and private enterprise. It's the dawn of a new China.' He bared his grey teeth, showing off a gold cap, as his gaze travelled up and down the girl's body. 'And what a China it is.'

Yangyang flushed but she didn't move. She planted her fists on her hips and glared, which only made the man grin wider.

Shaozhen stepped in front of her. 'That's enough.' His voice was deep, his brow pulled forwards. He threw his arm down and spat at the ground. 'Move along, you clod. We better not catch the likes of you in the village.'

The man shrugged and yanked on the donkey's rope. 'Suit yourself,' he said, with a final wink at Yangyang. Shaozhen thought the scowl on her face would burn holes in the man's back as he moved off down the road.

'What a disgrace. He's worse than a pig,' Shaozhen snarled.

'But what are we going to do?' Yangyang was clutching the front of her shirt, like she was still trying to hide from that lascivious gaze. 'Nainai still needs water.'

Shaozhen shook his head. 'I know. Come on, let's get a move on. The faster we get back, the faster we can give her water.'

The two struggled to lift the wheelbarrow again. It felt twice as heavy as when they had first set out. Yangyang's grip slipped and her side came crashing down.

'Sorry, Nainai!' she cried out. But the old woman didn't say a word, or even groan. She was out cold.

'We have to get her back to the hospital,' Yangyang cried, struggling to pick up her part of the load.

'That'll take too long. We're almost at the village – come on.'

Shaozhen heard a puttering sound coming from behind him. He whipped around to find Chun, pulling up on his moped.

'Thank goodness!' Shaozhen set the wheelbarrow down gently and waved to his friend. He barely had to raise his voice over the tiny engine. 'Chun! Quick. My nainai needs water. Can you get some from the village?'

Chun saw Nainai in the wheelbarrow, her eyes shut and head lolling to the side. He nodded and sped off without a word. Despite its unimpressive roar, Shaozhen was surprised at how fast the little moped could travel.

They resumed the walk, pushing their bodies to move as quickly as they could. They were going up a small hill now. His legs and hands burned, but Shaozhen bowed his head and kept up the pace, determined to get to the top.

It felt like eons had passed, but in the distance, they heard the low hum of the moped returning. Shaozhen sighed with relief and the two of them set down their load once more. Chun appeared over the hill and pulled to a stop beside them. He quickly extracted a small bottle of water from the bag on his back.

Shaozhen unscrewed the cap and held the bottle up to Nainai's lips. 'Nainai, please. You need to drink some water.' He was afraid to move her, to bring her to sitting, lest he aggravate her hip injury.

'Here.' Yangyang slid a blanket behind Nainai's head so she was propped against the side of the wheelbarrow. Nainai whimpered.

'Drink,' Shaozhen pleaded.

Slowly Nainai stuck out her long white tongue, probing like a donkey's. Shaozhen carefully poured the water. She caught a few drops, the rest sliding down the side of her mouth. In her hazy state, she smacked her lips, like she'd just eaten a big meal.

'Shaozhen.' Nainai's voice was weak but she was awake. Shaozhen heaved a sigh of relief and offered her the bottle again. Nainai pursed her lips and was able to get most of the liquid into her mouth this time.

Eventually, Nainai had drunk half the bottle and Shaozhen and Yangyang had even taken a couple of swigs themselves. The lukewarm liquid felt good going down Shaozhen's throat and it took all his control not to drink the rest. Instead he passed the bottle to Yangyang again.

'Thanks so much, Chun,' he said finally. 'You're a life-saver.'

Chun shrugged but Shaozhen could tell he was pleased to have helped. He shut off the engine and pushed the bike alongside them as they walked the rest of the way to the village.

It was quiet when they arrived. Most of the villagers were inside, probably preparing their evening meal. Shaozhen and Yangyang bid Chun farewell and hurried back to their house, keen to get Nainai into bed.

Kang was waiting by their front door. 'Hey, Kang! You don't have your nose in a book!' Shaozhen teased. Was he imagining it or did his friend have a guilty look on his face? 'We're just bringing Nainai back from the hospital.'

'I'll help you,' Kang said softly.

Together they put Nainai to bed. She moaned when they lifted her out with the sheets, but she fell asleep almost immediately, completely exhausted from the day's ordeal.

'I'll make us some dinner,' Yangyang said. 'Kang, you can stay if you want.'

Kang shook his head. 'Thanks, Yangyang. But I just need to talk to Shaozhen and then I'll go.'

They went outside. Shaozhen frowned at his best friend. 'What's the matter, Kang? You're acting strangely.'

Kang took a deep breath. 'I'm going to the city,' he finally blurted out, 'to be a migrant worker.'

'But you can't!' Shaozhen felt a ball forming in the pit of his stomach. 'You're not even sixteen.'

'I've already finished the required schooling. And we don't have money for senior school.' Kang dropped his head. 'My parents found me a factory job in Chengdu. They don't ask your age. They just pay you a salary in cash.'

He was speaking so fast that it was hard to catch all of the words pouring from him. Shaozhen was stunned. 'But you're – you're the smartest kid in the village. You're going to be a scientist. You'd get a scholarship to Beijing University for sure! And what about your grand-father? Who's going to look after the shop?'

Kang couldn't look him in the eye. 'My parents said there's nothing we can do. The shop makes no money. The harvest is dead. There's no water, there are no crops. Everything is dying in the village, even...' He let the rest of the sentence go unspoken, his face crumpl-ing into tears that he quickly wiped away. He stooped down to retrieve his backpack. 'I have to go. My parents called me today and said I have to get the last bus into Chengdu. I just wanted to make sure I'd said goodbye.' Finally, he glanced up and gave Shaozhen a grim smile. 'Hey, at least I can finally live with my parents. It was what I always wanted, right?'

Shaozhen felt something inside him breaking. He didn't know what to say.

Kang turned to go.

'Wait,' Shaozhen said finally. He hurried inside to his bedroom and rummaged under his bed. He found it tucked neatly between two basketball magazines; he had made certain to line it up perfectly so as not to crinkle the corners. He extracted it carefully and went outside.

'Here.' He handed Kang his limited-edition foiled Yaoming poster. It was one of his most prized possessions. He had always dreamed of going to Shanghai to have his idol sign it.

'Your Yaoming poster?' Kang's eyebrows shot up as he took the precious page in his hands. 'Are you sure?'

'You're going to Chengdu. You never know if he might do a special appearance. You can get him to sign it for us.' Shaozhen's eyes stung and he swiped brutally at his cheeks to hide the fact that he was clearing away his tears.

They gave each other an awkward hug.

Kang's eyes were big and round behind his glasses. He rolled up the precious poster and carefully tucked it into his backpack. Shaozhen watched his movements, not sure what else he could say. He tried to imagine what it would be like to be in Kang's shoes: a small, spectacled boy setting off to the city to work in a factory. Shaozhen's insides ached with heaviness.

Only when he could no longer see his friend on the path, did Shaozhen finally go back in the house.

Eighteen

Shaozhen was numb. Without Kang, it was as though the village had emptied. With all his time spent collecting water and working in the fields he hadn't seen much of his friend, but he had always sensed his warm presence close by. Now he felt like a part of himself was missing.

The next morning on his way to Xifeng, he passed the little shack that Kang had manned for his gung. It was still boarded shut, giving Kang's sudden departure an eerie finality. *No one's coming back* the shabby door and bent nails screamed.

Shaozhen went past Kang's house. There was an untouched plate of vegies covered with plastic wrap sitting on the stoop, a pair of kuaizi carefully laid on top. Shaozhen recognised those kuaizi from the few times he'd sat in Aunty Wu's kitchen.

The doors and windows were closed. He knocked gently. No answer. He pressed his ear against the door and heard a light wheezing and something else.

A sob? Kang's gung was in there, pretending he wasn't. Shaozhen felt an ache from inside. As much as Lao Zhu had pushed his grandson, scolded him and worked him to the bone, Shaozhen knew that he loved Kang. And now the old man was utterly alone.

Shaozhen let out a loud sigh and stepped away from the building. It was then that he spotted the two buckets and bamboo pole that Kang had carried on his tiny shoulders lying on the ground. Without thinking twice, he grabbed the pole and hoisted it onto his back. The poles were different shapes, which made carrying them both at once awkward. The buckets clacked together with every step, but he didn't care. With four buckets hanging from his shoulders, he set off for the town.

The queue was as long as ever and he waited nervously with his two sets of buckets, trying to avoid the eyes of the official overseeing the queue. Fortunately, the official seemed bored and less diligent than he had the first day the villagers had arrived.

As Shaozhen watched his second bucket filling up, he pushed the other pair into place. 'Two per household,' grumbled the driver. 'Them's the rules.'

'It's not for me. It's for my friend's gung. He…he's by himself now. His grandson left him. You remember Kang – the one with the thick glasses?'

The driver eyed him warily but relented and began filling the extra buckets. Shaozhen heaved a sigh of relief. Then he noticed a stack of empty buckets at the front of the truck and had an idea. 'Wait, can I have one more?'

The driver threw the hose to the ground. 'Are you *kidding* me?' The people behind him grumbled and Shaozhen felt his face go red. But he stood defiantly, and met the driver's eye.

'No, it's for old man Shen – you remember I was with him before? You've seen him. He barely gets a bucket a day. It's too little. Surely he's allowed his full share?'

The driver groaned but went to fetch a bucket. Finally, Shaozhen was left with four heavy buckets to balance and an extra bucket in his hand. He could barely walk, but he was determined to return to the village with his haul.

As he was making his way out of the town, a vehicle with a soft, puttering engine pulled up alongside him. Chun was doing his water run on the repaired moped. His two full buckets were balanced perfectly on his back. 'Hey, Shaozhen, what are you doing? Are you running a scam?'

Shaozhen tried to shake his head. 'It's for Kang's gung. And I got a bucket for the old man up the mountain.' He laughed. 'It seemed like a good idea at the time.'

Chun chuckled and shook his head. 'This is why Kang's got the head for numbers. Yours is a downright mess.'

They both laughed again. Chun killed the engine and climbed off the bike and they set down their buckets. The two stared at the seven buckets laid out in front of them.

Chun scratched his head. 'There has to be a way.'

It was like a torturous physics puzzle: how to balance the load and keep the bike from tipping over. Kang would know, but his ideas were usually theoretical, as though they had a jet-propulsion system and a world with no friction at their fingertips.

'There's no way to carry it all at once,' Shaozhen concluded. 'Maybe I could just wait here with the extra buckets for you to come back?'

Just then, there was a squeak of rusty brakes. 'What are you boys doing?' Tingming called out. The frame of his pushbike was too small for his burly form and the spokes groaned when he hopped off.

Shaozhen hesitated out of habit, remembering the way Tingming always taunted him on the court. Even after their stand-off with the man at the water queue, the two still weren't exactly the best of friends. But things were different now. *In times of hardship, we watch our brothers' backs.*

'We need to get this water to the village. That's for Kang's gung.' Shaozhen pointed. 'And that other bucket is for old Shen up the mountains. He can never carry enough water for himself.'

Tingming nodded. 'Wulei and I have been carrying water for the woman who lives next to us. She's completely bedridden and her grandson is only six. He cooks and cleans but he can't get the water.'

Shaozhen was surprised. He had always considered Tingming to be a bully. He'd never thought he would do something like carry water for his neighbour. 'Do you think you can help us carry some back?'

The older boy narrowed his eyes for a moment, as though contemplating the request. Shaozhen felt his face growing hot and he was about to tell him to forget it when Tingming picked up the buckets that belonged to Kang. 'I was here in Xifeng seeing if there were any jobs in the granary. But they sent me away.' He sighed loudly. 'I'll go see Lao Zhu,' he said.

'That'd be great!' Chun declared. 'And, Shaozhen, if you sit across the back of the bike and we balance the other poles across our shoulders with the last bucket between your knees, we should be able to take the rest!' Chun smiled like he had just figured out how to shoot rockets to the moon.

Tingming hoisted Kang's buckets onto his back and climbed onto his bike. The small tyres sank into the gravel and Shaozhen thought the bike might fall apart before their very eyes. But somehow Tingming got the gears to turn and the wheels to roll forwards, shakily at first but eventually with enough momentum to set a steady pace back to the village with his precious cargo for Lao Zhu.

Meanwhile, Chun fired up the engine. Shaozhen clambered onto the back of the bike, carefully placing one of the buckets between his knees. A small crowd leaving the water queue had gathered to watch their incredible balancing feat as they lay the poles across their shoulders, like stacking a house of cards.

'I always thought I could join the circus, you know?' Chun joked as they settled on the moped, their backs ramrod straight to keep the buckets from slipping.

'Balance and steadiness,' Shaozhen said, trying to limit his movements to just his facial muscles. 'Great for basketball. I'm sure this was part of Yaoming's daily practice routine.'

'I think he just shot hoops,' Chun replied.

The crowd was laughing and pointing now but the boys didn't mind the attention. Chun reached forwards and tugged gently on the handlebars. The little bike came to life and they very slowly set off. The machine strained with the extra weight but they managed to putt along at a slow but constant speed. It really did feel like a training session, a lesson in teamwork, with Chun shouting instructions to coordinate their efforts.

'Left turn coming up,' he called, and the pair leant gently into the turn and then straightened up.

'Gravel road up ahead.' Shaozhen tensed his legs to keep the bucket from slipping out from between his knees as his whole body vibrated from the bumpiness of the surface they were travelling over.

Finally, they arrived at the entrance to Hongsha. It took a fair bit of collaboration to extract themselves from the bike but finally the two boys were standing on solid ground with five relatively full buckets of water.

'That was great!' Chun grinned. 'We make a real good team.'

Shaozhen smiled. 'Thanks for your help.'

'Hey, do you want to take the bike up to the mountains to deliver the water to Shen? Just make sure to hide it before you start the climb.' Chun reached for Shaozhen's pole.

'Really?' Shaozhen was stunned that his friend trusted him with his precious motorcycle.

Chun nodded solemnly. 'We should do everything we can to help others in the village. Especially since our parents aren't here. We're all that's left.'

Shaozhen smiled. He knew what Chun meant. It was why he had picked up Lao Zhu's buckets in the first place. Even though he was missing his best friend and his parents, he didn't want to give up hope. His heart felt full.

Chun shouldered the other buckets. 'I'll take your water to your nainai, no problem. Come find me tomorrow morning. We can haul the water back for them together.'

Shaozhen climbed onto the bike. His smile was so wide, he thought his cheeks might crack in two. The bucket rested between his knees. He pulled very gently on the handlebars, half-expecting the bike to lurch out from under him and leave him behind. Fortunately, the controls weren't very sensitive. The engine growled like a jungle cat and as he coaxed the bike forwards, Shaozhen pulled a little harder and tucked his feet up onto the footrests. The front of the bike wobbled wildly but he tightened his grip and finally brought it under control.

Chun was right: the road to the mountain was short and smooth and it wasn't difficult, despite this being his first time riding a motorbike on his own. He arrived at the path to the mountain and brought the bike to a creaky stop. He got off and rolled the bike partway up the road then stashed it among the trees, using fallen branches to disguise it well enough that it wouldn't draw attention from the main road.

He set a brisk pace and it wasn't long before he came to Shen's little vegetable patch. The goat bleated, announcing his arrival. Shaozhen swallowed. He wasn't sure if old Shen was home or if he would come to the door after the angry blow-up he'd had last time they parted ways. But he reached up a clenched fist and knocked anyway.

Nothing. Shaozhen pressed his ear to the door. He could hear a faint shuffling from within, and then it stopped.

'Great Uncle Shen. It's me, Shaozhen.' He knocked again, harder this time. 'I have something for you.'

The rustling started again. Shaozhen waited. He was about to knock for a third time when the door squeaked open.

Old Shen peered out, his wrinkled face all twisted up and sour.

Shaozhen offered him the bucket. 'I, uh – I brought you some water, Great Uncle Shen. I – I know you don't *need* the help,' he added quickly. 'But the boys from the village and I, well, we wanted to help. We all wanted to do more for the villagers – I mean, for everyone.'

Shen narrowed his eyes and Shaozhen thought he was in for another verbal lashing. But instead, the man stepped out onto his stoop, his bony arm reaching out.

'Come inside, Shaozhen. Have a rest.'

Shaozhen smiled and carried the bucket inside.

Shaozhen was whistling, his tune loud enough to be heard over the sound of the bike's engine. He was tempted to *really* take the bike for a spin, but he didn't want to betray his good friend's trust. They needed each other. That was what he had come to realise most in these past few weeks. The village was a community. A superstar team better than the Houston Rockets!

He headed to Chun's house to return the bike then he set off home. But when he went past Tingming's house he heard voices. He recognised the husky laugh but the tinkling girlish giggle almost sounded foreign. He soon found their source.

Tingming was sitting on his front stoop with Yangyang, sharing a joke.

'Hey. Yangyang, what are you doing here?' Shaozhen approached the pair cautiously, sizing up the situation before him.

'Oh, hi, Shaozhen! Tingming stopped by looking for you. I said you weren't back yet and we got to chatting. He mentioned he had an unusual plant growing near his vegetable patch so I offered to take a look.' Yangyang's eyes were shining. 'You're very lucky, Tingming, not everyone can grow honeysuckle. Once the drought is over, you can expect some pretty flowers among your cabbage plants.'

'Is that…so?' Shaozhen couldn't mask the edginess in his voice.

Tingming stood, pulling his shoulders back so his chest stuck out. 'Wow, you're very smart, Yangyang.' The girl beamed, like she had just won an Olympic gold medal. Shaozhen tried not to roll his eyes.

'I was just returning Chun's bike. Thanks for helping with Lao Zhu's water,' he relented.

'No problem. I'm glad to run into you. I wanted to see if there was anything more I could do to help. You know, with the water-carrying,' Tingming said.

'Tingming said you and Chun were bringing water to the other villagers who aren't able to collect it for themselves!' Yangyang was practically bouncing on her heels. 'What a clever idea!'

'It is!' Shaozhen blushed when he realised how boastful he sounded, but he couldn't hide his pride. 'Well, I mean…I realised Kang's gung needed water and then there was Shen in the mountains and…well, Tingming and Wulei are helping their neighbour too…' He narrowed his eyes at Tingming once again. 'You really want to help?'

'I do.'

Shaozhen could see the calm sincerity in the older boy's eyes. Finally, he offered his hand and Tingming shook it.

Nineteen

Shaozhen was thrilled that Tingming, Chun and Yangyang seemed eager to help. Bolstered by their comments, Shaozhen asked his friends to meet him on the basketball court the next evening.

He paced nervously, practising free throws as he waited for everyone to arrive. Relief washed over him when he saw Chun, Tingming and Yangyang approaching.

'You made it!' Shaozhen high-fived his friends, even Tingming.

'Of course.' Chun smiled. 'And not just us, either!'

There were more voices coming from the road. Shaozhen saw Wulei and Chun's cousin Bo and they were joined by even more youths, boys from across the village, and even a couple of girls. They clustered around the basketball court, casting curious glances at Shaozhen.

Shaozhen was gobsmacked. 'What are you all doing here?'

'Everyone has been so worried about the drought and the harvest, but feeling helpless because all the adults are leaving,' Wulei explained. 'When we started talking, we all agreed we should be doing more ourselves.'

'We want to hear your ideas,' said one of the younger boys in the back. Everyone nodded.

Shaozhen took a deep breath. 'Well, I did think of something we can do for everyone.'

The group leant forwards, hanging on Shaozhen's every word.

'Instead of everyone bringing two buckets of water per family, we can bring water for the entire village,' he said. 'Our grandparents with their bad knees and hunch-backs won't have to trek out to Xifeng every day and villagers like Lao Zhu, who have been left on their own, will have more water too.'

Many of the boys were quick to agree.

'Kang's gung was grateful. I think he actually smiled. I don't think I'd ever seen Lao Zhu smile in my entire life!' Tingming said.

A few were less eager. 'Why should I help? With all the farm work to do and my own grandmother bed-ridden, I have enough work collecting water for myself,' one of the girls complained.

'The idea is that no one family will need to do more work than any other,' Shaozhen explained. 'If we all work together, each of us won't have to go to Xifeng every day and carry our own measly buckets home. We can bring more water for everyone in the village.'

But the girl was still not convinced.

'But what about the two-bucket rule? I tried to get an extra bucket for my neighbour once and that driver snatched it away from me,' she said. Others murmured in agreement.

The girl spoke again. 'Besides, even if we did try to carry water for everyone, we'd never be able to make enough trips in time. You only have one motorcycle. We won't be able to carry that much more than we already do,' she said.

'But you haven't heard the other part of my plan yet.' Shaozhen waggled his eyebrows in delight.

🌑🌑🌑

Shaozhen approached Xian's house. He hoped the Secretary was at home. Since queuing for water had begun, Xian had been spending most of his days in the Town Secretary's headquarters. The villagers whispered about it, wondering if their Secretary was avoiding them and speculating if Xian was on his way out like Luqiao.

Shaozhen's palms stayed damp no matter how many times he wiped them on his trousers and he felt a queasiness in his gut that was impossible to ignore. *This has to work.*

There was a single light on in Xian's oversized dwelling. Shaozhen hadn't been back here since he had asked Xian to drive Nainai to the hospital. He knocked softly on the grand double doors.

A weary-looking Xian appeared behind the slit of the open door. 'Shaozhen?' The Secretary's face was still thin and drawn and he had the same bags beneath his eyes.

'Secretary Xian, may I speak with you for a moment?' Shaozhen smiled, hoping he looked convincing, even though it felt as if there were grasshoppers in his stomach.

'Please, come inside.' Xian held the door open. 'Ah, forgive me if I don't…um…offer you some tea. In times of drought, we must all make sacrifices.'

Shaozhen gave a small, knowing smile and followed Xian into the living room. He was stunned to discover the TV was gone as well as the comfortable leather chair he'd sat in. Only the computer in the corner remained. 'They didn't feel right,' Xian said with a shake of his head. 'They weren't a reflection of who I wanted to be as a Village Secretary.'

They settled into the stiff wicker chairs, the only furnishings left in the room. There was a great expanse between them and Shaozhen felt like he would need to shout to bridge the chasm.

The pair both spoke at once.

'Secretary, I…'

'Shaozhen, I'm sorry…'

They laughed.

'Please, elders first,' Shaozhen offered.

'Shaozhen, I am deeply sorry. I don't think that I have done right by you and the villagers since I arrived. I – I made a fool of myself.' He hung his head. 'I wanted so hard to make an impression, to prove that what I knew and what I had learned could make great things happen, but I didn't listen to the needs of my own residents. The people I wanted to help. I am no better than your old Luqiao.'

Shaozhen felt bad for Xian. 'I – I think you're being hard on yourself. The villagers never liked the old Secretary, that's a given.'

Xian laughed. 'That may be so. But I want to make it up to you all. I've been working with Secretary Lam on some big ideas. That's why I've been spending so much time in Xifeng. Our plan, I think it will revolutionise Hongsha village and the Xifeng township, and hopefully help your families.' He looked Shaozhen in the eye. 'And, Shaozhen, I'd think you would be the perfect person to help me deliver the policy to the villagers.'

The boy rubbed the back of his neck, suddenly awkward. He didn't think he was ready to become a Party mouthpiece. 'Well, um, I actually came here because I wanted to talk to you about something. The boys and I, and Yangyang, too, want to do something for the village, something for all the villagers. But we need your help.'

'Oh? Go on.'

Shaozhen explained about Kang's departure. He talked about Kang's gung, Lao Zhu, and how he was too unwell to carry water. He told Xian about old Shen in the mountains.

'My grandfather's village in the mountains was lost to a landslide a while back. I didn't think anyone still lived up there,' Xian remarked.

'Old Shen does. And he's too stubborn to come to live in the village. He has to make the trip all the way to Xifeng for water. And I'm sure there are other villagers who are old and alone because their children have all left for the cities, like my parents have.'

169

Shaozhen paused to look Xian straight in the eye, trying to hide his nervousness before continuing. 'My friends and I think we should offer a free water-delivery service for the elderly. We'd visit them every day, and we could do chores around their house or the garden, and, of course, drop off the water. But we need your help. The town would have to give us enough buckets of water, not just the two-bucket limit, and we really need a vehicle – and *not* your personal ambulance service,' Shaozhen added with a half-smile.

To his relief, Xian laughed heartily. 'That was a bit silly, I have to say. I thought I was being a good Secretary by sticking to the rules. Secretary Lam heard about it and reprimanded me terribly. I – I have a lot to learn about the Party and its place in the community.'

Shaozhen's spirits soared like he had sunk the winning basket at the buzzer. 'So you'll help us? You'll lend us the truck?'

'Even better. I'll drive it.'

● ● ●

A few weeks later, a large group of youths were gathered at the entrance to Hongsha. What had started as just the Hongsha village teens getting water from Xifeng, had grown to include other teens in other villages as well. Boys and girls Shaozhen had only known at Xifeng Junior Middle School and a few that he had never seen before because they hadn't gone to school were all helping out. The villagers were calling them 'water-carriers'. There were pushbike-pedallers and wheelbarrow-draggers, all coming together to help. Their numbers kept growing and now there were thirty-odd water-carriers from across the region.

Shaozhen, Chun and Tingming came out and greeted the boys with high fives while Yangyang headed over to the huddle of girls. Many of the teens were left-behind children, just like them, and they had all become fast friends.

'You boys up for a game of basketball tonight?' Shaozhen asked. 'We can get a full game going, I reckon.'

'Hey, we'd love to, but harvest starts tomorrow,' said one of the boys from Weiying village, two li over.

Shaozhen's eyes lit up. 'Wow, really? We're not starting ours until next week.'

'Yeah, we're going to try and save what we can. Won't be much, but a harvest is a harvest. You know, we could use some extra hands. I don't know if—'

'Of course we can help!' Tingming said. 'This is what the water-carriers are all about. Villager helping villager, village helping village.' He glanced at Shaozhen, who gave the older boy an affirming nod.

'Make way! Make way!' The group of teens dispersed as the vehicle approached the entrance to the village. Secretary Xian stuck his head out of the window, a look of intense concentration on his face as he swivelled the truck in between the two lines the water-carriers had formed, like feeding a soccer ball between the goalposts.

Xian caught Shaozhen's eye and gave the boy a small triumphant smile as the team swarmed the truck. Shaozhen flashed the Secretary the thumbs up.

Chun hopped up onto the back of the truck and began passing pails of water into the waiting hands of the teens below them.

'Feiyuan from Weiying missed her delivery yesterday. Do you think she can get an extra bucket today?' someone asked.

'Wangpeng from Shunmiao said he won't need a second bucket today, so she can have his,' Chun said, handing the water-carrier his extra load. 'Be careful, that one's really full.'

'Tingming, will you carry this for me?' Yangyang appeared to be struggling with a bucket, even though Shaozhen had seen her carry loads three times that weight without breaking a sweat. He rolled his eyes but said nothing. Tingming didn't seem to notice anything amiss and took the extra bucket without a word.

They all set off in pairs or trios, some with wheels, most on foot, to deliver the water to its intended recipients.

Xian hopped down from the truck and picked up an extra bucket. 'Shaozhen, I'll come with you to visit old Shen. You've told me so much about him, I'd like to finally meet him in person.'

Shaozhen shook his head. 'I don't know, Secretary. Shen doesn't really take kindly to visitors, especially from the village.'

'I'll take my chances.'

The pair were quiet on the walk up to Shen's home. Xian began to whistle, not a revolutionary song but a pop tune from the radio, and a love song at that. 'I would never have picked you for a Luhan fan,' Shaozhen chuckled.

'The lyrics are good,' Xian said with a shrug. Over the past few days, Shaozhen had noticed a change in Xian: he was more like the Xian who had played basketball with them on his first day in the village. Instead of the pained look of a weary Village Secretary, Xian looked young and happy.

Shaozhen was on edge as they passed the garden plot and approached the house. Shen had come to accept Shaozhen's daily visits and had even stopped insisting he didn't need charity. While he wouldn't say the old man had *warmed* to him, he was less callous.

The goat bleated as usual, announcing their arrival.

'Shaozhen, are you ready for another lesson?' Shen was setting up the Chinese chess pieces on a small stool at the front of the house. They had played one game before and Shaozhen had lost miserably. Shen stopped halfway through laying out the king pieces when he looked up and noticed the Secretary.

'Who is this?' he demanded, glaring harshly at Shaozhen.

'This is Secretary Xian from Hongsha village,' Shaozhen mumbled. He could tell from the venomous change in Shen's expression that he shouldn't have brought Xian here.

'What do you want? I have no business with you, the Party or Hongsha,' the old man snarled.

Xian held his hands up in peace. 'Please, Comrade

Shen. I mean you no harm. I just wanted to talk to you. I know about Mao.'

Shen squinted at the young man. 'How do you know about Mao?'

Shaozhen's ears perked. *Who's Mao?*

'My grandfather was from Xiaosong.'

A gloominess settled over old Shen's features. 'Leave Mao to rest in peace. Bad enough I had to bury my children, but a grandchild too...'

Shaozhen furrowed his brow. 'I thought your children died in the famine.'

'His sons and wife passed during the Three Bitter Years,' Xian answered for Shen.

Shaozhen was stunned. How did Xian know this? The boy tried to meet Shen's gaze but the old man turned away.

The Secretary went on. 'But Shen had a daughter. She married a man from Xiaosong, a farmer she loved dearly. But he never felt good enough for her. His family was very poor. So when a bunch of men came to the village offering a fast and easy way to make money, he thought it was a sign from the heavens.'

Shen was staring at the ground, his toothless jaw trembling.

Xian continued. 'So this farmer, along with some of the other villagers, sold his blood. He convinced his wife to do it too, as often as once a week. They built a new house with the money they earned. And then they had a son.'

Xian's voice softened. 'But soon, many of the other

villagers fell gravely ill. The blood drive had caused a sickness, something that had never been seen before. And before long, the farmer and the new mother were very sick too.'

Shaozhen stood there, his mouth agape. He knew without Xian telling him how the villagers had passed, why they were sick. Since Shaozhen had been a boy, there were whispers of ghostly villages throughout the province that were marked for death, stricken by a deadly and vicious illness.

Aizibing, AIDS.

'The Party did nothing,' Shen whispered. 'The villagers begged for help but the Party let them die. Another footnote to be written off with slogans and propaganda. It's all your fault.' He pointed a trembling finger at Xian but then he let his hand fall, too weary to even hold it up. 'The villagers drove the sick out.'

Shaozhen looked from Shen to Xian, the pieces slowly falling into place. 'Your grandfather was the Party Secretary of Xiaosong,' Shaozhen said finally.

Xian nodded. 'He was. He witnessed the villagers getting sick, so many people needing help. But there wasn't anything he could do. The hospitals were full and he suspected the medicine they gave him to distribute was nothing more than sugar pills.' He bowed his head. 'He couldn't bear to watch. He was heartbroken, so he quit his post and moved his family to Wuhan. And that's where I was born. He never spoke of the tragedy that befell the village of Xiaosong, but I knew it was the cause of the heavy weight he carried in his heart.'

'Your grandfather left and the village was in chaos.' Shen pressed his lips together, like he was trying not to cry.

Shaozhen's heart was in tatters. Shen had lost his wife and sons to the famine and his daughter to AIDS. 'What happened to their son?' he asked Shen.

'After my daughter and her husband passed, the little boy was on his own. He was just three years old but no one in the village would take him. The sick families had all been driven out and no one wanted to take in a sick boy. The entire lot of them shunned a helpless child because they were afraid of his illness. They treated him worse than a dog.' He banged his fist against his palm, his puffy eyes fierce and angry. 'So of course, I took him. I couldn't bear the possibility of him suffering at the hands of the Hongsha villagers like he had in Xiaosong, so I left my home in the village and came up to the mountains on my own. I built this house. I planted a garden to grow food and I raised the goat for milk. I taught my grandson numbers and how to read, all by myself. And we were happy for the short life he had.'

Shen fell silent. His face looked weary and worn out, like he had somehow aged ten years in ten minutes. He slumped down on the ground beside the stool with an enormous weight that sent the chess pieces clattering to the ground.

Xian bowed deeply three times. 'Lao Shen, on behalf of my grandfather, the Party, the villagers and the people, for what it's worth, I apologise for your great loss.'

Shaozhen bowed deeply beside Xian so that his forehead was practically touching his knees. He was full of anger and sorrow. His misgivings and sadness about his parents leaving was nothing compared to Shen's suffering.

There was a long silence and then Shen sighed and stood up, wiping his face with the back of his hand. 'Begone, you two. You'll have more water to deliver to the others. I know you boys have set up quite the enterprise.'

They turned to leave. But Shaozhen had one more plea.

'Great Uncle Shen,' he said softly. 'I know the villagers don't understand your suffering and I see now why you don't want to associate with us. But the harvest is coming. It's been a rough year for everyone, there has been little water and the crops aren't much. But the villagers in Hongsha are planning to celebrate anyway. Because sometimes, even in the worst of times, we need to try to be happy. I think – I think you should come.'

Xian didn't say a word, but he nodded in agreement.

Shen's face was unreadable. But Shaozhen thought he might have seen just the tiniest, most imperceptible nod. And that was enough.

Twenty

Harvest time arrived. And just like every other year, the villagers came together to work on each other's fields in the spirit of village togetherness. Everyone pitched in to pick the ears of corn by hand, even the children. They worked in teams of ten, traipsing up and down the rows with straw baskets on their backs and hats on their heads. Shaozhen worked with Yangyang and Tingming, the three of them weaving through the plants, plucking the ears of corn.

Once all the corn for one family had been picked, the group moved to the next field, while a few of the men stayed behind to cut up the plants to be dried for straw.

The harvest was minimal. Many of the ears of corn had not reached full maturity because of the drought; their kernels were white and stubby instead of bulbous and full of milk. Some of the stalks weren't even worth sifting through because they were so meagre.

But despite the sparse crop, the villagers still worked hard, preparing the land for the next planting. They laughed and shared jokes and sang songs as they picked the tiny ears of corn and placed them dutifully into the baskets that hung around their shoulders. They harvested through the long morning until Aunty Law and Aunty Wu came by with homemade buns to hand out for lunch. The workers were all famished. They set their tools on the ground and wolfed down their meal.

The harvesting and land preparation went on late into the evening, until it was too dark to see.

The villagers toiled through the next couple of days, their muscles aching, their joints stiff and wooden from the repeated motions. Shaozhen was so tired and worn out that he could barely keep his eyes open. Even Yangyang was too exhausted to give Shaozhen a hard time.

The good news was that Nainai was sitting up now, which meant she probably hadn't broken her hip. Shaozhen and Yangyang were exceptionally relieved. She couldn't work in the fields, of course, but she tried to keep up a cheerful mood.

'My precious grandson, you have become quite the farmer. Your grandfather would be very proud of your rugged peasant spirit.' She surprised him one evening by taking his hand in her own. His fingers were almost as hard and calloused as hers now, proper farmer's hands. She turned his palm up and tickled the centre. 'Your parents and I want you to have a good future, Shaozhen. And the future of the village isn't on these farms. If only we could change our circumstances.' Her eyes were brimming with tears. 'We wanted you to go to school, you know? To be a scholar and to graduate from university, like your friend, Kang.'

'Kang's not in school anymore, Nainai. He went to work in the city.'

Nainai sighed and shook her head. 'So it is. Even the most promising peasants cannot escape their fates.'

●●●

Their brief harvest ended just days before the Mid-Autumn Festival. The crops were all gathered and packed, and a few trucks had taken away the corn to be sold. The money was doled out to the farmers. Yangyang and Shaozhen proudly collected their share for the Lu family plot. It wasn't much, certainly not as much as he remembered Ma and Nainai collecting last year, but Shaozhen felt extremely proud of every last fen. They had worked hard for this.

'Your father and mother would be so proud of you,' Nainai told him. Shaozhen grew solemn, but he was surprised that his heart didn't seem to ache the way it usually did when his grandmother mentioned his parents. He missed them badly, but he found he was less sad.

Despite the pittance, the villagers were happy and livened as they prepared for the Mid-Autumn Festival celebrations.

On the day of the festival, Shaozhen found Xian at his door. The Secretary had a long roll of paper tucked under his arm.

'Secretary Xian, this is unexpected. What brings you to our humble home?' Nainai was up and about, hobbling on a cane.

'Lu Po.' Xian bowed to the old woman. 'It's good to see you walking.'

'Yes, Wang Daifu said it was a good idea to do a bit of walking around to strengthen the muscles again. Just you wait – I'll be back out in those fields in no time.'

'That's wonderful to hear.' Xian smiled. 'I think you might like what I have in store, then.' He unfurled the papers. 'And, Shaozhen, I'm counting on you and the rest of the boys. And Yangyang as well,' he added when he saw her hovering by the door.

Curious, they all gathered around the cramped folding table as Xian laid out the large sheets. Shaozhen recognised them as the kind of plans used by carto-graphers and archivists. But these weren't drawings of anywhere he could immediately recognise.

Yangyang pointed at one of the sheets straightaway. 'This is Hongsha. And here's the stream, and here's the road to Xifeng.'

Shaozhen was impressed.

'That's right,' Xian said, 'and this is the plan that Secretary Lam and I are going to put forward to the rest of the municipality.' He pointed to a large area marked with boxes and grids. It took a while for Shaozhen to realise that the scratches were buildings and roads – big ones, at that.

'The new Hongsha,' the Secretary said. 'There'll be a health clinic, a senior school and a water pump for every residence.' He indicated a section in the middle. 'Here will be the new headquarters and more shops. And a factory and mill for people to work.'

Shaozhen was speechless. The drawings before him looked clean and felt very real. He ran his finger over the large L-shaped factory, traced them along the lean double-lane roads. Could they really build a new Hongsha?

'But where is this new Hongsha going to go?' Nainai was peering over their shoulders.

'I'm glad you've asked this, Lu Po. The Party will be compensating the farmers for their land and providing new accommodation to move into. It'll bring construction jobs for your families, so there'll be greater opportunity at home.'

'But you're taking our land?' Nainai's face dissolved into a scowl. 'That's where our ancestors are buried, including my husband. That land has fed us for all these generations, and I'll be damned if I'm going to be handing our blood, sweat and tears over to the government again!'

'Laobo, please.' Yangyang laid a gentle hand on the old woman's shoulder. Nainai looked perplexed and conflicted.

Xian seemed embarrassed and started to roll up the pages he had brought. 'I'm sorry, I didn't mean—'

'Nainai,' Shaozhen interrupted, addressing his grandmother, 'I'm sorry you feel this way. After the last few months, I've realised how much the land means to you, how hard you've worked, and everything you have sacrificed to keep us alive.' He took his grandmother's trembling hand. 'I know you and Yeye went through so much and suffered greatly. But after all those hardships, maybe now is the time for you to rest. Let us, the younger generation, look after you. Let me help you.'

His grandmother's eyes started to water as Shaozhen went on. 'I'm not a good farmer by any means, but I can probably work in a factory. Maybe even go to school. I want to take care of you at home. I don't want to leave you behind and go to the city. What Xian and the Party suggest…maybe this way, boys like me can have a job and still be a part of Hongsha.'

Xian gave a formal bow. 'Lu-sum, the community of Hongsha has survived thanks to everything your generation has done. I know you see me as only a mouthpiece for the Party, but I really do love this village. And I want to do everything I can to help it thrive in the future, so you can have a long, deserved rest and your grandson can prosper.'

Nainai squeezed her eyes shut, holding back tears. She grabbed then kissed her grandson's hand. 'You're a good boy. You're a very good boy.'

Shaozhen choked back tears of his own.

'And you're a smart lad.' She shook a finger at Xian. The Secretary lifted his shoulders, clearly pleased with the remark, as though Nainai was his own grandmother. 'You too, Yangyang. A real smarty. Your generation…we older folk might have underestimated you. China is in good hands.'

'So, you approve of the new policy, then?' the Secretary asked hopefully. It seemed important that he received the old woman's endorsement.

'If my grandson sees it as the future, then I approve of his foresight.'

Xian nodded, relief reflected in his eyes. 'I'm so happy to hear it. I'll need the villagers' support, you, the headmaster, Wang Daifu and more. It might be hard to get the funds from Beijing but I am determined to try. What use am I as a Secretary if I can't help shape a better future for my village?'

'You're a good Secretary, Secretary Xian.' Shaozhen copied Xian's formal deep bow. And they all laughed.

❀❀❀

That night, the village of Hongsha threw an incredible feast. They set up makeshift tables on the basketball court, using plastic bags as tablecloths and buckets and basins as stools and tables. Dishes were brought out from the houses for all to share – some hot, some cold. Shaozhen had become so used to eating pithy vegetables for every meal that he couldn't believe his eyes. In spite of the drought, the village had managed to put together an impressive impromptu traditional water banquet featuring soups of all tastes and varieties. 'This will definitely bring the rains!' Mongsok joked.

Everyone sat down to take part in the feast, even Nainai, who under Wang Daifu's care was carried out and given a prime seat at one of the tables.

Shaozhen felt his mouth flooding as he watched the first dishes being laid out on the table, mudanyancai. Not made with actual swallow's nest, such delicacies were beyond the means of a humble village like Hongsha, but

Shaozhen was sure Aunty Law's cooking could rival a top city chef. He was about to tuck in when he spotted a figure approaching the group, slow and uncertain.

It was old Shen.

'Great Uncle Shen!' Shaozhen abandoned his seat and headed for the old man. Xian was already there, smiling and leading Shen to his table and offering his own seat. At first glance, Shen appeared to be scowling but then Shaozhen saw the moisture in the old man's eyes.

'Shen Yeye!' Xiaoping launched himself into the old man's lap and clutched his small arms around Shen's thin frame. That broke him; Shen sobbed, letting the tears flow.

'Welcome home, Shen,' Aunty Wu said beside him as she poured his tea.

They all toasted the harvest. They toasted each other for surviving the drought. And finally, when they were just about ready to dig in, Xian raised his mug one more time.

'And we toast the water-carriers.'

Shaozhen smiled at his friends. It had been a long summer. His mother and his best friend were gone but he had made some new friends as well. He raised his cup, his eyes seeking out Chun, Tingming and finally coming to Yangyang by his side.

He felt at home.

They ate and ate well into the night under the brightness of the stunning mid-autumn moon. They chatted and laughed and swapped stories and tall tales. They commiserated and harmonised and later, after a bit of baijiu, white alcohol, that Mongsok had kept stashed away, Shen even sang while Aunty Wu, Aunty Law and Nainai joined in. Song and Xian smiled and clapped each other on the back, congratulating the other for a job well done.

The moon was high in the sky when the last of the villagers staggered home leaving just Shaozhen and Tingming on the basketball court. The women had already cleaned up and most of the villagers had gone to bed. Shaozhen had helped Yangyang take Nainai home, but he wasn't ready to sleep. He was buzzing with excitement from the feast as well as the plans that Xian had shared. For the first time since he'd returned to Hongsha after his exams, Shaozhen felt happy and hopeful.

Shaozhen marvelled at the fullness of the moon in the cloudless sky. It looked extra big, like a sugar candy hanging from a sliver of thread.

'So, have you heard from Kang?' Tingming asked.

Shaozhen nodded. 'Xian let me use his computer. We tried a video call but it was too slow so we used a chat app. Kang has a mobile phone now. But he says he hardly has time to use it. He just works all day long.'

'I guess life in the city is still really tough.'

'Did the job offer from Zhanfu come through?' Shaozhen hoped he wouldn't have to say goodbye to another friend so soon.

The older boy shook his head. 'It looks like I'll be staying in Hongsha this year. But with all the talk about the new Hongsha, maybe it won't be so bad.'

They sat in silence. Despite the lateness of the hour, Shaozhen was still bursting with energy.

Tingming must have felt the same way because he turned to Shaozhen and said, 'How about a quick game of one on one?'

'You're on!'

The pair weaved and threaded the ball between them as they darted around the basketball court. The sounds of celebration from the night had been replaced by the rhythmic slap of the ball and their panting breaths as they sank into the familiar thrill of the game. They played well into the night and the birds were awake when Shaozhen finally fell into bed, weary but happy.

And, at long last, the next morning the rains finally came.

Author's note

China is a vast country, brimming with diverse people, culture and experiences. I grew up in New York with Chinese parents who did everything they could to instil in me a deep appreciation for my heritage: celebrating Chinese New Year with gusto and bravado, and regaling me with stories based on longstanding traditions. But even with my background and upbringing, I'm still learning new things about China and its people every single day.

Despite the images of towering skyscrapers, smog and booming industry, China as a whole is a largely agricultural nation. According to the National Bureau of Statistics of China, about 45 per cent of its almost 1.4 billion inhabitants are still considered to be living in rural areas. In 2010 a lack of rainfall in China's Northern, North-Eastern and Central provinces meant that farmers had to rely heavily on irrigation or risk losing their crops. At the time newspaper headlines proclaimed that this was the 'worst drought in 50 years'. But just a few years later, the region would once again be crippled by a water crisis that would have villagers and city-dwellers alike struggling to find water for their day-to-day needs.

In 2014 this region, known as China's 'Northern Breadbasket', suffered an even worse drought, devastating harvests throughout the provinces of Sichuan,

Shanxi, Beijing Municipality, Hubei, Shandong, Inner Mongolia, Jilin, Liaoning, Shaanxi, Fujian in the south and Shaozhen's home province of Henan. Without water, people's livelihoods were in great peril. *China Daily* reported that the drought had affected over 4 million hectares of farmland, that an estimated 35 per cent of Henan Province's small reservoirs had completely dried up, and that half of the small- and medium-sized rivers that were essential for irrigation had stopped flowing.

Of course, the impact of the water shortages on actual families is more complex than can be presented in charts and figures. As I started looking into Shaozhen's story, which began as an investigation into the effect of the drought, I came across more and more startling information about the empty villages in China's countryside. These villages had almost no residents of working age and were inhabited largely by the elderly and children – children who were 'left behind' to be raised by their grandparents while their parents sought work in the city. In a country where rules of mobility and residency are determined by hukou, many migrant workers found they could not take their children into the cities without the right permits. In the cities, their village offspring would be denied medical treatment and education, all of which were tied to the residency system. As farming life became more and more difficult, children were increasingly 'left behind'. And with the demanding and gruelling schedules that most migrant workers were forced to keep, many children only saw their parents once a year, during Chinese New Year.

Reading some of these 'left-behind' children's devastating stories broke my heart, but it also gave me plenty of room to explore the tenacity and resilience of the younger generation. Shaozhen and his friends learn to rely on each other. What's more, they realise that by taking on some of the roles and responsibilities of the absent adults they can effect change and have a positive impact on their community. While the characters, along with the village of Hongsha and the township of Xifeng, are fictional, the experiences are real. Left-behind children are doing their best to find their way in an adult world without their parents to guide them.

In the non-fictional world of things, China's landscape is rapidly changing. While the cities find themselves unable to support the influx of migrant workers from rural areas, the government continues constructing new cities and urban developments throughout China's rural heartland at an incredible rate. In researching and writing *Shaozhen*, I was stunned by how different today's China is, compared to the one my parents emigrated from so many years ago. The impact of modernisation on China's agricultural backbone is staggering and its final effects, good or bad, are still to be determined. But if there's one thing my parents have always said about our homeland and ancestry it's that given the country's turbulent and colourful past, the Chinese people always adapt to change.

Timeline

2014 June China Meteorological Administration forecasts the first El Nino event in five years will hit north and central China by midsummer. The reduced frequency of typhoons causes major drought concerns for the wheat, corn and soybean production areas in the north that account for over 50% of the China's GDP and water usage.

July The worst drought in more than 60 years affects millions of people and 4 million hectares of farmland, cutting agricultural and domestic water supply in several provinces including Henan, Hubai, Shandong and Liaoning. Rainfall totals in central China are down by 21% from the previous year.

Henan Province receives only one-third of its 2013 rainfall total and 35% of its small reservoirs are dry. Daily temperatures in the province exceed 37 degrees Celsius. Drought threatens to end eleven consecutive years of annual growth in China's harvest and exasperate China's long-term water crisis as more

than half of the country's 50 000 rivers
are now dry.

August Key northern breadbasket provinces,
Henan and Inner Mongolia struggle with
the record-breaking drought. Summer
rainfall is 60% below seasonal averages.
China Radio International reports
economic losses of $1.2 billion in Henan
Province with crop devastation advancing
at a rate of 153 333 hectares per day.
Climate change, over-exploitation of
resources, historic low groundwater levels
and pollution are contributing to the
severe situation. Almost 330 000 people
in northeast Liaoning Province are without
sufficient drinking water.

September Domestic water supplies are
severely affected as groundwater levels
hit historic lows in northeast and central
parts of China. Henan reservoirs become
so dry that car washes, swimming pools
and bathhouses in the city of Pingdingshan
are closed.

Heavy rainfall finally ends
record-breaking drought. Provincial
drought relief headquarters in Xinhua,
Hunan reports an average of 49 mm of
rainfall has fallen over six days, lifting the
total storage of Henan reservoirs by more
than 200 million cubic metres.

December China launches the central route
of the $62 billion South-North Water
Transfer Project, a multi-decade project
of 2400 km network of canals and tunnels
to divert 44.8 billion cubic metres of
water annually from the Yangtze River in
southern China to the Yellow River Basin
in northern China. Farmers living on
the outskirts of the targeted cities can no
longer gain access to groundwater, vital for
their domestic needs.

2015–2017 Despite the project's promise,
north and central China continue to
wrestle with a long-term water crisis.
Government solutions include a push
for greater reliance on water-intensive
imported goods such as grains and oils.

Dry weather affects Hebei, Henan
and Shaanxi provinces despite heavy rain
events in Inner Mongolia. New varieties of
drought- and pest-resistant hybrid corn are
providing some hope to farmers.

Glossary

aiyah ah; cry of alarm and surprise

aizibing AIDS

ba father

baijiu Chinese alcoholic beverage made from grain; literally 'white wine'

baobei nickname meaning 'baby' or 'treasure'; precious one

bendan insult meaning 'fool'

chunjuan spring roll

cong spring onion

Dabaitu popular brand of lolly; literally 'big white rabbit'

dage big brother; also 'ge' or 'gege'

daifu doctor (traditional form of address); see also 'yisheng'

fen smallest unit of currency

ganshu sweet potato

gege big brother; also 'dage' and 'ge'

gung; gong maternal grandfather

huangdouya soybean sprouts

hukou official residency system in China that determines your level of access to various public facilities and is generally determined by where you were born, not where you live

jie big sister; also 'dajie' or 'jiejie'

kuaizi chopsticks

lajiao chilli

laoba old man; an informal way to address an elderly man (like 'gramps')

laobo maternal grandmother; see also 'popo' and 'waipo'

li half a kilometre

ludou green beans

mahjong popular tile game

maque sparrow

mudanyancai Henan soup dish, traditionally made from swallow's nest

muhuolu wood-burning stove

nainai paternal grandmother

niu ox

popo maternal grandmother; an informal way to address an elderly women; also 'po'

roujiamo meat pancake; common street food in the provinces

sanlun popular form of transport in regional China that resembles a three-wheeled motorcycle; also 'sanlumotoche'

shugong great uncle

siyuyan insult meaning 'dead fish eyes'

sum ma'am; an informal way to address a middle-aged woman

tubao; tubaozi insult meaning 'country bumpkin'

wah wow; used to express surprise

waipo a formal way to say maternal grandmother; see also 'popo' and 'laobo'

xiaomaibu corner store

yeye paternal grandfather

yisheng doctor (more modern form of address);
see also 'daifu'

yuan standard unit of currency

yucai traditional cooking of the Henan province

Find out more about...

Henan province

https://www.britannica.com
Search for 'Henan Province China'

2014 drought in China

'Severe drought in Henan, China affects thousands',
CCTV News, 26 July 2014
Search for 'Severe drought in Henan' at
http://america.cgtn.com/

www.chinadaily.com.cn
Search for 'Drought persists in central China's
Henan province'

The South-North Water Diversion Project

'Water diversion project to tackle northern drought in
China', *CCTV America*, 15 September 2014
Search for 'Water diversion project' at
http://america.cgtn.com/

https://www.theguardian.com
Search for 'China's water diversion project starts to
flow to Beijing'

The left-behind children

'China's "left-behind" children', *BBC News*,
12 April 2016
Search for 'China's left-behind children' at
www.bbc.com

'Generation Left Behind', *Foreign Correspondent*,
ABC TV, 6 September 2016
Search for 'Generation Left Behind' at www.abc.net.au

www.abc.net.au
Search for 'A generation left behind: Millions of
Chinese children abandoned as parents seek work'

Acknowledgements

This book proved to be a delightfully beautiful challenge for me to write and conceive.

I have to thank my parents for their insights and my husband for his endless support. Special thanks to Kay and Roger for their helpful perspectives as well as bits with language. (And a shout out to my hometown of Flushing, Queens, where I was first introduced to the regional cuisine!)

My deepest thanks to the very talented Lyn White for inviting me to contribute to her very successful and valuable series. I am exceptionally honoured to be taking part. Finally, my heartfelt gratitude and appreciation goes out to Eva, Sophie, Jess and the team at Allen & Unwin for all of your extraordinary hard work, patience and keen eye for detail.

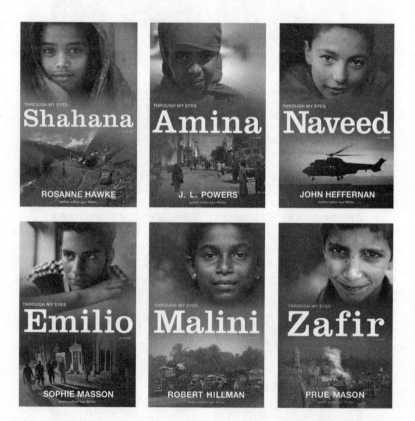